DISOWNED

John Duncklee

Pipers Willow, Inc.
Sheridan, Wyoming

DISOWNED

by John Duncklee

Published by:
Pipers Willow, Inc.
Sheridan, Wyoming

ISBN: 0-9787277-3-8

ISBN-13: 978-0-9787277-3-4

Library of Congress Control Number: 2007921913

Cover Art by Penny Duncklee

Cover Design and Typeset by Jaspal S Bisht at Aruna Enterprises, D-2/39-A, Dayal Pur, Karawal Nagar Road, Delhi-110 094, India. E-mail: jpl@rediffmail.com

Printed in the United States of America.

For information, write to Pipers Willow, Inc., 1617 N. Main St., Suite B, Sheridan, WY 82801.

DEDICATION

To My Wonderful Wife, Penny

CHAPTER ONE

Carlos Montoya and his two brothers, Juan and Pedro, sat on one of the plank benches in the Mesilla plaza. They stared at the adobe courthouse where inside, fifteen minutes before, a judge had declared their ownership of the San Ignacio de Toluca land grant invalid. The judge signed a deed to Steven Preston, a Texan from the San Antonio, Texas area. The brothers sat shocked and numbed with disbelief that the Americans would do such an act against them.

Carlos remembered the day he had ridden into Rinconada with a packhorse to get some supplies for the ranch before roundup began. The town was abuzz with the news of the Gadsden Purchase. Everyone wondered what life changes would come with the Americans in charge of what had been part of Mexico. Carlos felt disowned by Santa Ana when he heard that the former general, turned president, had sold the 45,000 square miles of Mexico to the United States for $10,000,000 dollars in gold. One day Carlos was Mexican, the next he became American, and it had not been by choice. In many ways he felt abandoned, lost, and skewered by the announcement of the Purchase posted on the wall of the presidio where Mexican troops remained to keep the peace. That is, if one could call it peace when the Apache raiders continued to kill and plunder at will.

Everything had been going well on the San Ignacio de Toluca grant. Everything had always gone well there as long as young Carlos could remember. Certainly there had been droughts, raids by Apaches and rustling by cattle and horse thieves, but all that was part of the life on the ranch. One Apache raid had caused near annihilation of the Montoya family. Challenges were expected and there seemed to be solutions to just about everything that happened to intrude or interrupt the normal trend of life until the Mexican troops vacated Rinconada and the American flag got hoisted on a makeshift flagpole in the presidio. That was when Carlos, and his brothers Pedro and Juan, had spent the better part of two years with anguish, fear, uneasiness, and uncertainty trying to find a solution to what they considered a total injustice to the Montoya family.

After the Gadsden Purchase, the Texans began arriving. The common expression to describe them was "men riding fast horses and carrying long ropes". It seemed to the old timers that the Texans arrived quickly and in great numbers in their quest to acquire land and cattle. They came with a lust for rangeland to replace what they had ruined in Texas by years of overgrazing. Some of the Texas judicial people accompanied them. Before Carlos and his brothers knew what was happening they had been called into court in the territorial capitol of Mesilla next to the Rio Grande River, far from Rinconada. There they heard the Texan judge tell them that they no longer owned the San Ignacio de Toluca because the deed was flawed and that Mister Steven Preston would be moving into the headquarters within six months. The judge told them that he was sympathetic to their plight and would allow them those six months to find another place for their cowherd or sell it.

After the court session, bewildered at the turn of events and still trying to understand what had happened, Carlos and his brothers looked up with surprise as Preston approached them. “I can take your cows off your hands,” he said, chewing on a matchstick.

“I expect you would enjoy that, Señor Preston,” Carlos said. “Then you would have everything that the Montoyas have worked for since Spain owned this country.”

“I can’t help it if you didn’t get your deed legal,” Preston said.

Carlos Montoya decided right then that selling the family cowherd to the Tejano would be a good idea regardless of the price. Cattle meant cash, one thing the Montoyas never had much of. There were too many Montoya mouths to feed and the ranch was almost the total source of the family livelihood. Most of the clan lived at or near San Ignacio de Toluca. Those who lived elsewhere made separate livings but had always depended on the ranch to supplement their income. Only one family member, Rugerio Montoya, uncle to Carlos, Juan and Pedro, had gone to Rinconada and worked as a wagon maker. After ten years of frugal living and money from the family, he had set up his own shop and had prospered.

“When do you want to look at the cattle, Señor Preston?” Carlos asked.

“I will be back in Rinconada in a month. You name the day.”

“I will try to get some samples gathered for your inspection, and send word to you.” Carlos said.

“I ‘ll be staying at The Glover,” Preston said. “Do you mind if I bring my foreman?”

“Bring anyone you want with you, Señor Preston. Nothing matters anymore. We will wait for you at headquarters. Will you need saddle horses?”

“That depends on where we have to go to see the cattle. I will be driving out in a buggy. If you think I will need saddle horses, we can tie them onto the back of the buggy until we need them. Both my foreman and I have our own saddles.”

“Until then, Señor Preston.”

“Until then, Montoya.”

Preston left the Montoya brothers sitting on the bench. When he was well out of earshot, Juan asked, “Carlos, why are you going to sell our cattle to that Tejano cabrón?”

“I knew you would ask that question. I thought about it quickly. I almost told him to go piss up a rope, but then I had an idea. We sell the Tejano cabrón our cowherd and then we steal them back and drive them across the border where some of our relatives still have ranches. Our brands are still in Sonora as well as here in New Mexico Territory.”

“Will this work?” Pedro asked. “Suppose the Mexican policía arrests us for cattle stealing?”

"I thought about that, too," Carlos said. "We will have plenty of cash from the sale of the cow herd to the pinche Tejano and we can pay the Mexican officials some mordida, the old fashioned bribe that always serves well in Mexico. And it was not so long ago that San Ignacio de Toluca was part of Mexico."

Carlos sat thinking about when they had become citizens of the United States of America, and locally of New Mexico Territory, by a notice nailed to the bulletin board on the wall of the presidio. The old familiar political centers of Arispe and Pitic were no longer the centers of law and politics. He recalled his grandfather's story about how the Montoyas had obtained the San Ignacio de Toluca Grant from the King of Spain, before Mexico had won its independence. He remembered the story about the long ride his great grandfather had made to file the papers in Arispe before the United States was even a country of its own. Now the distance to Mesilla was three times as far as to Arispe.

In spite of their grant of land, the Montoyas had never been considered part of the hacienda level of Mexican society. The grant was too small to be of major significance, and too small to allow the family to live in a large town or *pueblo* and manage their holdings in absentia. Then came the drastic change in citizenship that gave them cause to worry about their future. If a collection had been taken among the entire family they would not have enough money to hire the right lawyer to protect their title to San Ignacio de Toluca. They had heard about other former Mexicans being driven off their land holdings by the Texans and others with strong desires to establish large cattle empires. There was even one large ranch owned by three British gentry called “The English Boys”. The Montoyas worried, but hoped the land grabbers would pass them by. “We are people without a country,” Carlos said to his brothers.

The Montoyas never felt the same after Mr. Gadsden made his purchase making them citizens of the United States whether they wanted to be or not. They could have gone south and remained citizens of Mexico, but the San Ignacio de Toluca was now entirely in the United States of America. They felt like they no longer had a country to be loyal to and to look to for protection against Apache raiders and others. Why did the government of Mexico sell them out? They did not belong anywhere.

Adding insult to injury, they had suddenly become second-class citizens because their skin was brown. They felt the cut of Tejano prejudice.

In spite of the spattering of genes from a Spanish padre at the mission in San Patricio, Carlos’s Yaqui and Opata ancestry determined his short stature of five feet five inches. He tried to overcome that “gift” by riding as straight in the saddle as he could when he was around others. He had never been to San Patricio and his only knowledge of it had come from his grandfather before he passed on to wherever old men go when they die. The strongest memory he held about that village was what his grandfather had said about finding a shaman in San Patricio if he ever needed help. San Patricio was the small pueblo the Montoya family considered their place of beginning. Ever since he heard the judge's decision about the change in ownership of San Ignacio de Toluca, the words of his grandfather kept battering Carlos's mind.

Carlos had just celebrated his eighteenth birthday when his grandfather, Ysidoro Montoya, an old man with snow-white hair and stubble of white beard, called him over to sit with him on the old bench under the big mesquite tree in the barnyard by the well. It was the old man's favorite place on the entire ranch. Nobody ever sat on the bench without a personal invitation. Later, when the old man died, the family moved the bench to the cemetery that had started with the land grant. They placed it next to his grave that, like the others, had a mound of rocks on top of it to discourage coyotes and other scavengers from digging.

Ysidoro's message to his grandson had lasted nearly an hour. He told the boy about his experience as a young man going to San Patricio to visit a shaman and learning about datura, the devil weed that the Texans called Jimson weed. The spreading plant had large, dark green leaves with huge, sweet smelling, white flowers shaped in a cone and round, prickly seedpods. He also mentioned peyote, or Mescalito. Ysidoro said that he learned much from the shaman and that if ever Carlos felt the need to experience a different outlook on the world, he should travel to San Patricio where the Montoyas began as a family. "I told your father about San Patricio, but I think he will not go there for some reason," Ysidoro said.

Carlos enjoyed having his grandfather's attention, but wondered why the old man had not told his younger brothers about San Patricio. It was not long after the conversation with his grandfather that the old man took Carlos and his brothers hunting deer and javelina in the foothills of the mountains. They came back to San Ignacio de Toluca with the pack mules laden with two deer and three javelina carcasses, a successful hunt, but a sorrowful return. Apaches had raided the headquarters, stolen all the horses and killed everyone except Carlos's mother, who lived just long enough to describe what had happened. Carlos had felt as if his world had come to an abrupt end. Grandfather sat in silence on his bench for a day and a night holding his grandsons after they had buried the dead in the family cemetery. In one swoop Carlos lost his parents, his sister, an uncle, aunt and two cousins. It took over a year for him to recover enough from the massacre so that the memories of the dead were no longer constantly swimming across his mind.

Besides his two brothers, Ysidoro was the only close relative alive, and he spent more and more time each day sitting on his bench rather than ride with his grandsons husbanding the cow herd. When Carlos informed him about Mexico selling the northern part of the country to the gringos, Ysidoro merely shrugged his shoulders and muttered something about nothing remaining the same anymore. Seven months later Carlos and his brothers placed him in his grave in the family cemetery next to his beloved Mariana, who had passed on two years before the Apache had made their disastrous raid. Carlos had wondered if his grandfather was happy to finally join her.

Preston and his foreman, a Texan named Holt, arrived at San Ignacio de Toluca at mid-morning. Carlos showed them the horses they could saddle and with that done he and Juan accompanied the new owners of the grant out into the hills to view a sample of the cowherd. Carlos knew where the cattle would be until shortly after noon. He led the men to a waterhole known as Tanque de Coyote. It was at the mouth of a canyon that drained a small mountain range to the West and held stock water even during severe drought.

Arriving at the waterhole, they saw the cattle lying under the shade of mesquite trees that lined the banks of the streambed. Disturbed by the sudden presence of humans, the cattle rose, looked intently at the intruders and then began to mill around as the riders reined in their horses and remained on horseback to inspect the cattle. There were close to a hundred head of cows with about fifty calves already born. Some of the cows bawled at their young to make sure they were close by. Several began to move their heads back and forth showing their nervousness near humans.

"Have you seen enough, Señor Preston?" Carlos asked. "I have more to show you and it would be best to leave these mother cows to finish their morning by the waterhole."

"Nice looking cows. Have you ever bred them to Texas bulls?"

“No, all the ranchers around here have always tried to keep the Andalusian blood as pure as possible. Our cattle seem to be as thrifty as they come and can make a living during drought as well as in times of plentiful feed.”

“I haven’t seen any two or three-year-old steers,” Preston remarked as they rode toward the next waterhole.

“I have already shipped them. Last winter’s rains were scant so I sold the two-year-olds along with the three-year-olds to save feed.”

“That means I will have to wait two years before I can sell anything,” Preston said.

“That is better than running out of range like you Tejanos do back in Texas.”

“We raise a whole lot of cattle in Texas.”

The cattle had begun to drift back onto the hillsides when they arrived at the next waterhole. Carlos led Preston and his foreman through the cows and yearlings that remained. Then they rode into the hills to see what they could find before heading back to headquarters. At the corrals they unsaddled the horses and strolled over to the main house where they sat at the kitchen table sipping coffee brought by Carlos’s aunt, Rosa. They began with small talk about cattle in general and then got down to the business at hand.

Preston argued for market price and Carlos insisted that cows already located on the range were worth more than just any cow. Just as Carlos got ready to tell Preston to forget about buying the Toluca cows, the Texan gave in to

Carlos's price. Then, Carlos made one stipulation to the transaction; "Señor Preston, there is one more thing I will ask for," Carlos said.

"What do you want, next year's calves?" Preston replied.

"I want a paper from you that allows any member of the Montoya family to visit the family cemetery that is on the hill behind the headquarters. We also want to be able to continue to use it for those of us who pass on. We may not be able to stay here in life, but we would like to remain here with our people after life."

"I will arrange for that as soon as I return to town," Preston said.

"I suppose all there is left to do is to is gather the Toluca herd, tally them, and then settle our business." Carlos said.

"You still have close to six months to stay here," Preston said.

"It will take at least a month to gather the cattle because they are scattered from here to the far end of the valley. We will have to separate them from all the neighbors' cows. That all takes time and a lot of work. There are a few wild ones in the high country that we might have to count from a distance."

"When are you figuring to start the gather?"

"I will need a week to get the word out to the neighbors so that they can participate. Then, they will need a few days to get their work caught up to free them for the gather. Let us plan on starting two weeks from today."

"That sounds agreeable to me," Preston said.

Two weeks later to the day, twenty-four riders assembled at the Toluca headquarters, ready to begin the gather to tally the cattle. Some of the men were ranchers, others were cowboy representatives. Preston and his foreman drove up in a buggy as the rest watched with a curiosity that might have been taken for contempt. Every one of the neighbors was aware of what had happened and they all wondered if their holdings would meet a similar fate at the hands of the new law of the United States. Some had dismounted while others remained in their saddles as the two Texans saddled the horses that Carlos had hitched to the rail outside the corrals. Nobody spoke. They had already expressed their anger.

When Preston and his foreman were mounted, Carlos told everyone his plan for the gather. He explained what areas they would work and who would ride where. Once the cattle had been assembled at specified points, they would separate the Toluca cattle from the others and count them. Each Toluca animal, cow, calf, yearling or bull would have its tail bobbed once Carlos and Preston had put them in the tally book.

Pedro Montoya, the youngest of the brothers, had the responsibility to bring Rosa and the midday meal to the gather point in the buckboard. Juan stood ready to ride with Carlos to help with the tally should the Texans question the count or procedure. The sun had just spilled into the valley when the riders started riding away from headquarters to the far away mountains.

They spread out and made a long sweep over the eastern slope of the mountain. By the time the sun cast its shortest shadows the riders had assembled some four hundred head in the canyon known as Garrapata, or Tick. Pedro and Rosa arrived earlier with the food and started a cooking fire. The kettles contained ample supplies of beef and beans. The large coffee pot stood filled with fresh brew on some coals that Pedro scraped away from the fire. Rosa heated the freshly made tortillas on an iron plate called a *comál*. Leaving four cowboys to keep the herd intact, Carlos invited the rest to the meal. The first four to finish, mounted their horses and returned to relieve the others so they could satisfy their hunger.

Carlos spoke to one of the ranchers named Sandoval. "Enrique, on Hermano Ridge near the top, I spotted an orejana that I remember seeing on one of your cows when she was a calf. She's a long yearling with a peculiar brockled face. I couldn't get behind her in the sweep so I left her there. Tomorrow morning I can take you there and with some help and we might be able to burn your brand on her."

"I think I remember when she was a calf and wild as a deer," Sandoval said. "Thank you for letting me know where she is."

When Sandoval mounted and rode off toward the herd, Preston said to Carlos, "We call those unbranded cattle "mavericks" in Texas. Why don't you burn your own brand on that heifer as long as she's a maverick?"

"Señor Preston, we work closely together on this range. Sandoval would have done the same for me had the situation been reversed." *Even the ethics would change with the Texans*. Carlos thought to himself.

Once everyone had eaten, Pedro and Rosa loaded the buckboard and headed back to headquarters. The others cut out Toluca cattle to count and have the tassels on the ends of their tails cut off so they would not be counted twice in case they were brought in again during the gather. A cow can travel a good distance overnight.

There were several unbranded calves with their mothers. Taking advantage of the gather, the owners heated their irons and burned their marks into the hides of the youngsters. One of the calves belonged to a Toluca cow so Carlos put his brand on it. Carlos and Preston counted a hundred twenty-seven Toluca cows that first day. Back at headquarters, some of the neighbors who lived farthest away spent the night in their bedrolls in the bunkhouse. The others rode home after learning where Carlos planned to gather the following day.

They worked the north slope of the mountain the following day. Carlos led Preston, Holt, Sandoval and two other cowboys up Hermano Ridge to see if they could find the unbranded heifer belonging to Enrique Sandoval. They arrived earlier than the day before and there was no sign of the wild one. "Let's check the seep up at the head of Garrapata Canyon," Carlos suggested. "She might be there at the waterhole."

They rode further south to the headwaters of the canyon. When they neared the waterhole, Carlos held his hand up to stop the riders. "I will ride in close and try to see if she is there. Wait here. I will whistle if she sees me and tries to make a break for it into the piñones."

Carlos rode slowly toward the spring, hunching over to make himself less conspicuous. The unbranded heifer looked like she had been at the waterhole for some time. She had stretched out under a large piñon, and was chewing her cud. Carlos reined the buckskin gelding slowly around, glad that the heifer was not facing them. Back with the riders, he explained the situation at the waterhole. "If we can surround her while she is relaxing, we might be able to start her down Garrapata Canyon. Once at the bottom, she will be tired and one of us should be able to throw a reata around her horns."

The group spread out to surround the heifer. The mountain country challenged them with its rough terrain and steep slopes. Carlos thought about the steep sides to Garrapata Canyon and felt reasonably assured that they could keep the heifer to the bottom until they came to the mouth of the canyon where they had worked the preceding day.

Carlos watched the heifer rise quickly to her feet once she heard the horses climbing around on the rocky ground. She darted her head from left to right at least four times before she snorted and headed away from the sounds of the hooves. Just as Carlos had hoped, she began trotting with her head still darting back and forth from left to right. The riders closed in. "Enrique, take the south slope, I will ride the north just in case she tries to climb out of the canyon." Carlos called. "Señor Preston, you and your foreman can bring up the rear in case she decides to turn back to her mountains. Sandoval and I will try to meet her at the mouth of the canyon where we worked yesterday."

"All right," Preston called back.

All went well until Carlos and Sandoval reached the mouth of the canyon and began riding up to meet the wild, unbranded heifer. As soon as the heifer saw the two riders she stopped dead in her tracks. She looked around for an escape route and returned her stare to Carlos and Sandoval who had reined in their horses to wait for the heifer's next move and for the others to close in from upstream. Their reatas were both made into loops ready to throw should the heifer try charging past them. Again she shook her head and snorted. The men could tell she was both angry and afraid after being disturbed from her normal routine.

Carlos saw the riders closing in from behind the heifer. She glanced around and decided that her best chance for freedom would be to charge the two riders in front of her. Leaping forward with her eyes darting back and forth toward the two riders, she began her charge, heading between them. Carlos reined the buckskin and spurred him at the same moment to slow the heifer's momentum by blocking her route. The heifer dodged and for a second Carlos thought he had lost her, but he sent the loop of the reata singing toward her head as she fled. Seeing that he had her horns caught in the loop, Carlos pulled back on the slack and had a tight loop capturing the heifer. Quickly wrapping the reata around the horn of his saddle in a dally, he began reining in the buckskin as Sandoval rode swiftly over to the heifer's rear and threw his reata to catch her hind legs. Another good shot. The two stretched the heifer until she dropped to the ground. Carlos dismounted quickly and began tying her hind legs first. Then he jumped around the thrashing bovine until he had all four legs manacled tightly with his long piggin' string.

As the others rode up, the two Mexican cowboys smiled at the captured orejana and began gathering wood for heating the branding iron that Sandoval handed them from his saddle.

"Pretty good rodeo, no Enrique?" Carlos said.

"Maybe we should try our luck the next time they have one in Rinconada."

"That might be too difficult to do without Garrapata Canyon for an arena."

The irons heated soon and Sandoval branded his animal with his mark. They released the angry heifer and she high-tailed it up the canyon. They continued gathering cattle, tallying the Toluca animals and branding any calves they found that had escaped the spring work. The gather took close to three weeks before all the neighbors and Carlos felt they had covered the country as best they could. Carlos thanked them for their help and as he said his good-byes he wondered if he would ever again join his friends gathering cattle. He had only felt worse the day he had learned about the deaths of his parents and sisters at the hands of Apache raiders. The end of the gather meant the end of life, as he had known it.

He and Preston retired to the house, where they washed away the dust from their throats with a shot of mescal. Then, they compared their tally books. "Señor Preston, I tallied one thousand twenty four cows, eight hundred forty-two yearlings and ninety bulls. What are your numbers?"

"I counted two more cows, four less yearlings, and the same number of bulls."

"Around here we figure we miss ten percent," Carlos said.

"What are you trying to tell me, Montoya?"

"There are still uncounted cattle that we missed and should be included in the total."

"That sounds quite out of bounds to me," Preston said.

"How do you do things in Texas?"

"Pay on the tally is all I ever did."

"This country is probably quite different than you are used to. Do you have mountain country or rolling hills?"

"Pretty much rolling hills where I ran cattle."

"Then you should understand what I am talking about when I say we figure missing ten percent when we gather like we did. If we went back over the country again, we might find the rest and then again we might not."

"I am not sure I agree with this," Preston said.

"Perhaps you would rather I sell the cows elsewhere," Carlos said, losing patience with the Texan. "You got my ranch for nothing so now you think you can get the cattle cheap."

"Now, hold on, Montoya. I got the ranch fair and square. The judge ruled on it."

"That does not mean much to me. Do we have a deal on my cattle or not?"

"I suppose I can afford the extra ten percent even though I think you Mexicans think you are too clever."

"Shall we finish the business in Rinconada, Señor Preston?"

"We will have to because all my money is in the bank there."

"Before we do that, would you be interested in buying the Toluca horses?"

"I might, but I need to look at them."

"We can ride out to see them in the morning."

"That sounds fine. How far do we have to go?"

"The stallion generally keeps his mares up in Mariposa Canyon. One of the neighbors said he saw them there a week ago when he was driving some cows down from the mountain."

Early the following morning, Carlos and Preston saddled up their horses and headed for Mariposa Canyon, a two-hour ride unless the weather was nasty. The fall sun came up in a clear sky. A crisp breeze met them as they neared the foothills of the mountains.

Carlos reined in his horse before going up the trail that led to the rim of Mariposa Canyon. "We should be able to see them once we have passed through the foothills," he said. "Viewing them from the ridge above the canyon is easier than trying to get close to them on the canyon floor. The stallion would have them charging away up the mountain before we got close enough to see his sweethearts."

They started the climb over the first of the foothills to a point where the canyon walls became steeper. The trail led them back away from the rim for several hundred yards. Suddenly, Carlos reined in his horse and looked intently toward the canyon. "I smell smoke," he said without taking his eyes away. "There it is. Follow me and we will see what kind of a fire we have here."

Preston followed Carlos toward the canyon rim. Arriving at the edge, Carlos held his hand up, signaling Preston to stop. Carlos dismounted and looked down into the canyon, then bent over and led his horse back to where Preston waited. "Apache warriors," Carlos whispered. "I counted eight of them roasting one of my colts. The head and hide were on a rock near the fire."

Carlos mounted the bay gelding. "We had better get out of here. They are probably heading for Mexico or they would have driven off all the mares and foals."

Just as the words came whispering out of Carlos's mouth an arrow thunked into the chest of Preston's gray gelding. The horse reared squealing, throwing the Texan to the ground. The gray thrashed around for a moment before life left it still on the ground.

Carlos took his left foot out of the stirrup. "Get over here, Preston. Climb on back."

Preston limped over, put his left foot in the empty stirrup and vaulted up to a position behind Carlos. "What about my saddle?" The Texan asked.

"Dead men do not need saddles. If we don't get moving quickly there are at least nine warriors who would enjoy seeing us dead."

Another arrow whizzed by them, missing whatever target it was intended for, and lodged itself into a clump of sagebrush. Carlos, his left foot back in the stirrup, spurred the bay into a plunging run down the trail. Under other conditions he would have kept his horse to a walk to traverse the narrow, steep grade.

Arriving at the bottom of the trail, Carlos kept the horse moving. After a quarter mile he slowed the bay and looked around to see if the warriors followed. "The one who shot at us must have been a lookout," he said. "I probably could have killed him if he hadn't shot the gray."

"What are you going to do?"

"Señor Preston, I am going to get us both back to San Ignacio de Toluca. I doubt if the Apache will follow, but I do not try to outguess those cabrones. They killed both my parents and my sister. I do not like giving them a horse or two, but I do not think it wise to try to stop them single handedly."

"I have heard about Apache raiding, but I never thought I would have a horse shot from under me by one," Preston said.

“Consider yourself fortunate that the arrow got the horse instead of you,” Carlos said.

“I wish we could have seen the mares before all that happened.”

“We can go back up there tomorrow. Those devils will most likely be far away by then. Once they know they are discovered they do not stay around. They will feast on that colt and be gone by nightfall.”

“Why don’t you notify the army so they can go after the raiders?”

“By the time I ride to Rinconada and get a chance to talk to the army those Apache devils will be far into their mountains.”

The next day Carlos and Preston rode up the same trail as before. When they arrived at the spot where the lookout had shot the gray gelding, they saw what remained. The Apache had taken much of the hindquarters but left the rest for the buzzards who flew away in a flurry of loud flapping of wings when the men arrived at the scene.

“They took my saddle,” Preston said.

Carlos rode over to the rim and looked down. “They are gone,” he said. “We might as well get going up the canyon because the stallion might have taken the mares clear to the top of the mountain after those cabrones killed that colt.”

The two men rode further up the trail, Carlos peering over the side intermittently to see if he could see the mares. After an hour of uphill climbing they came to a point where the canyon became shallower. Soon it began to be joined by smaller steams, several of which carried streams of clear water. Carlos stopped to give his horse a chance to quench his thirst. Preston did the same.

"Look at the tracks," Carlos said, pointing down to the ground. "The mares have been here this morning. I will bet that stud took them up to the piñon country."

"Wherever he took them, we should be able to follow their tracks," Preston said.

They rode further up the mountain through juniper and a few piñon. Carlos saw the stallion first. He stood on a knoll above a grass-covered area that had been burned a few years back. The mares had fanned out and were grazing. Foals nursed their dams. The stallion gave forth a loud neighing. The mares lifted their heads and looked toward him.

"We better try to get behind the stud," Carlos said. "If we can get them all headed back down to the canyon we can drive them back to headquarters."

"I just need to look at them for a moment," Preston said. "I have never bought a horse without seeing him first."

"There should be fourteen mares and six fillies. I wean and halter break the colts when they are eight months old. Those are down at headquarters. You may have seen them in one of the corrals when they came in for water."

"Yes. They looked like good horseflesh. What am I going to have to pay you for these mares?"

"Ten dollars and forty for the stallion. I will toss in the fillies and the colts."

"Do you mean I don't have to pay for ten percent more than we see here?"

"The stallion keeps his mares together. Bulls breed the cows, get them pregnant and are on their way," Carlos said, ignoring what Preston obviously considered humor or sarcasm.

They returned to Toluca headquarters, spent the night and then started for Rinconada the next morning, arriving in the evening. Preston drove his buggy while Carlos followed on the bay gelding. Preston's foreman had returned to Rinconada right after the gather on a horse he borrowed from Carlos.

Preston went to the Hotel Glover. Carlos rode to his uncle's house, after agreeing to meet with the banker the following morning. He felt strange to be on the eve of selling the Toluca cowherd and the mares. Wondering about what the next stage in his life would be, he chatted with his uncle about the prospects of the freighting business since the latter flourished in his wagon-making enterprise. Before retiring for the night, Carlos strolled away from the residential section on Sixth Street toward the center of town where the cantinas stayed open all night.

After finding a place at the bar in the Lucky Dollar, he ordered a mescal. When the burly barkeep brought him the shot, he tossed it down quickly and asked for another. The second went down as easy as the first. He thought about drowning his thoughts in mescal, but decided that he did not want a hangover in the morning when he had to keep a sharp eye on the Texan and the banker.

Walking back to his uncle's place he kept thinking about what had happened, getting angrier by the minute. *I suddenly learn that I am no longer a Mexican, but an American. The only other choice is to move south to Mexico, but my home, my ranch is now part of the United States just because some gringo named Gadsden paid Mexican politicians for land no matter who lived on it. I became a foreigner in the land of my birth. The Tejanos began moving in. Then, a judge tells me that I no longer own San Ignacio de Toluca and I sell the livestock to a Tejano who I can barely stand to talk to. Tomorrow morning I am supposed to get the money for the livestock at the bank. I do not want money. I want the ranch. It is my home. It has always been my home. One of these days I must ride to San Patricio and find the shaman who my grandfather spoke about. But, I do not want to move to what is still Mexico.*

He fell asleep shortly after going to bed. Nightmares kept waking him and when he got out of bed in the morning he felt as if he had not slept in days. At breakfast, Carlos said nothing. His uncle looked at him several times. Carlos could not speak for fear he would begin weeping. Anger and sadness overwhelmed him.

He left his horse in the corral behind the house and walked the ten minutes in the brisk air of the fall morning to the center of Rinconada. The Territorial Bank maintained its office on Main Street once called Calle de Anza after the Spaniard who had founded San Francisco.

Carlos had been inside the bank several times and maintained an account with William Barlow. Preston sat in one of the leather chairs in front of the banker's desk. Barlow rose and greeted Carlos with a handshake. "Steve tells me you two are here to finish a cattle and horse trade," Barlow said.

Carlos did not smile or even look toward the Texan. "Here are the figures," Carlos said, pulling a slip of paper from his jacket pocket.

Barlow took the paper and compared it to another that lay in front of him. "Since you are both in agreement, we might as well get this settled so you two can go about your business. The easiest way to handle this is for me to transfer funds from Steve's account into yours, Carlos."

"That sounds fine with me. All I need is a receipt from you, Señor Barlow."

Barlow wrote out a receipt for Carlos, handed it to him, and turned to Preston. "I can arrange for annual or semi-annual payments," he said.

Carlos paid no attention to what the banker had said as he scrutinized the receipt before putting it into his pocket. He left the bank feeling hollow, empty and robbed. In spite of the early morning hour he headed for the Lucky Dollar where he spent an hour with mescal.

Before heading back to the ranch, Carlos stopped by his uncle's wagon works to say good-bye. As he mounted the bay gelding for the return trip, Preston and his foreman, Holt, rode up together.

"Montoya," Preston said. "Since the cattle and horses are paid for, I assume I am now responsible for them."

"They are your cows now, Señor."

"Mr. Holt and I are wondering if you and your brothers would stay on to help us. I will pay top wages."

Carlos almost told Preston that Montoyas never worked for wages. Then, he had an idea. If they were going to steal the cattle back, it would be good to have someone at the ranch that knew what was going on.

"I will ask them as soon as I get back," Carlos said.

"Good. We will stop by in a couple of days to find out their decisions. What about you?"

"I will stay for a while to show you what you can expect from the country and the livestock. However, I must get started doing something to make my living without a ranch."

"I hope we can count on all three of you," Preston said.

"As I said, I will ask them as soon as I get back to the ranch."

The brothers, along with the four ranch dogs, rushed out from the house and met Carlos as he rode into the barnyard that evening. They sounded anxious to hear what had transpired at the bank. Carlos told them that everything went all right and that the money was in their deposit account.

"How would you like to stay on here and work for wages for Preston?"

"I am not sure about that," Juan said. "That would mean working for Holt and he does not seem to be friendly."

"When are we going to steal back the cattle?" Pedro asked.

"I have not had time to think about that, little brother," Carlos said. "But when we do it will be easier if we have someone on the inside telling us what is going on. One thing I have thought about is that we should steal the steers after they gather them and save ourselves some work. For one thing, the yearlings will not be ready for market for two more years. We should let Preston take care of them for those two years, no?"

CHAPTER TWO

Carlos surveyed the village of San Patricio as he rode along the narrow dusty road edged with eroded adobe dwellings with sod roofs and crooked, glassless window frames. The wood, weathered gray and dry-rotted from the intense sun, seemed at the end of life just as the village. A scraggly hen missing her tail feathers scurried across the road in front of him, followed by an equally scraggly rooster. Some of the houses bragged with potted geraniums or other bright colored flowering plants in earthen pots hanging from the exposed, round, log vigas with rawhide strands.

The village reflected the drought that pervaded the entire southwest. Carlos had never seen a drier year. During the ride south he saw withered trees, brown, powder-dry grass-es that lacked enough moisture to grow seed stalks. On top of that, a continual desiccating wind sucked dry a puddle from the gelding urine in minutes, leaving an alkaline crust around the edge where the moisture had been just moments before. Carlos sought the shade provided by an ancient mesquite tree that had seen a lifetime of dry years interspersed with a few bountiful rainy seasons. He rested until evening, then mounted the gelding again for the last leg of the journey to the house of the shaman in San Patricio.

He came to a corner where a young boy, wearing tattered remnants of a shirt and pair of trousers with the knees worn through, stood scrutinizing him. He reined in the roan gelding. “Hola,” he said.

The boy turned away. The turn was not a quick movement, but one that told Carlos that the boy did not ordinarily talk with strangers. “I am Carlos Montoya from San Ignacio de Toluca,” Carlos said.

The boy turned back to face him. “I am Febronio Montoya,” he said. “Are you a cousin?”

“I must be if your name is Montoya.”

The boy relaxed now that he knew he was talking with someone who was not a complete outsider. “How can I be of service to you?” Febronio asked.

“I am here looking for a shaman. My grandfather told me about his visit here many years ago. He told me about the village shaman and now I have come to see him.”

“I know the shaman. He lives beyond the end of the village near the mesquite bosque. Follow me, and I will show you his house,” he said, and smiled showing a row of white teeth.

“Lead on cousin,” Carlos said, and smiled back at Febronio.

Carlos reined the gelding around the corner. As before, houses lined both sides of the road and when there was an occasional alley between houses, he saw a variety of animals living in the corrals behind the dwellings. The few horses he saw were thin with drawn up flanks that told of the lack of feed. Thin, sad looking hogs sniffed around the dirt, trying to find some sort of morsel to grab in their teeth. *This is not a happy place. Now I can understand why Great Grandfather left for the north.*

Just beyond the rows of small houses, an open plaza that looked abandoned opened to a crumbling adobe building that still held on to its dome and steeple even though the walls looked likely to fall at any minute. *The mission church. That is where the Montoyas got their Spanish blood. It hasn't been a church for a long time.*

"What happened to the padres?" Carlos asked.

Febronio stopped and turned toward his cousin. "I do not know. There have never been padres there in my life, only the old building that is falling down."

Another hundred yards and Febronio stopped again and turned toward Carlos. "This is as far as I can go. The shaman's house is around the curve up there," he said, pointing. "Be careful of the shaman's dog."

"Thank you, Febronio. I hope we meet again, soon."

"I hope so, too," the boy said, and turned to return to the village.

Carlos continued around the bend and soon an old adobe house, surrounded by a fence made from ocotillo, came into view. The place looked deserted until a mangy looking floppy-eared dog came trotting out of the yard, barking in such a way that it seemed to Carlos that the animal had mustered all his strength to do his duty. His age showed in the generous supply of gray hairs around his muzzle and the scattering of them through his dirty brown coat that may have never been shiny. The dog's ribs clearly showed and there was a yellow substance in the corners of his eyes. *I hope the shaman is in better shape than his dog.*

Carlos reined the gelding to a stop in front of the sagging gate, also made from ocotillo stalks lashed to a frame with rawhide. He remained mounted.

Moments later the front door underneath a porch opened and a small, wiry looking man with shoulder length gray hair stepped outside and stared at his visitor. His loose fitting shirt flapped in the breeze and the huaraches on his feet looked like they had always been there. His trousers were threadbare in the knees. Carlos looked at the man's calloused hands, and then up to his face that had the tough country written on it with wrinkles that varied from deep to hairline crow's feet at the corner of his eyes. His eyes had a faraway look in them that Carlos had trouble understanding.

"Hola," Carlos said.

"Who do you look for?" the shaman said.

"My grandfather, Ysidoro Montoya, sent me to find you," Carlos replied.

The shaman hesitated and took his spindly, sparse chin whiskers between his thumb and index finger of his right hand. "Ysidoro. A long time ago. He is from San Ignacio de Toluca."

"Yes, that was my grandfather."

"You said 'was'. Does that mean he no longer lives?"

"Grandfather passed on three years ago. He told me to find you if I needed to look at things clearly. He mentioned datura and Mescalito."

"I am acquainted with devil's weed and Mescalito.

He became their friends, too. What is it that is bothersome for you?"

Carlos related what had happened concerning the Gadsden Purchase and his change in citizenship and the loss of the ranch. However, he did not go into the plan to steal the cattle back.

"Put your horse in the corral. We must talk more so that I understand where you walk," the shaman said. "Did you bring food?"

"I have a little left in my saddle bags."

"You will need to go out and get food for both of us once we have decided what we must do. I will tell you what to get because you may be away from here for some time."

Carlos led the gelding into the corral where an old burro stood over in a corner under a shade tree. Returning to the porch he saw that the shaman had brought out two old wooden chairs with ladder-backs and well-worn, woven wicker seats.

"Did your grandfather tell you my name?"

"Yes. Diego Vasquez. I am Carlos Montoya."

"My father was also a shaman. He was Manuel Vasquez. He was one half Yaqui and one half Opata. He taught me."

"How long does it take to see clearly?"

"That depends on the person. Datura and Mescalito act differently and in different ways on different people."

Carlos said nothing, waiting for the shaman to continue, but he seemed to have finished talking and took a cornhusk and filled it with tobacco rolling it into a cigaro. He took a match from his shirt pocket, struck it on the leg of his chair and began smoking. He finished the smoke and continued looking toward the sky over the ocotillo fence. "You must learn patience," Diego said. "To have your own datura plant will take a year. Datura will teach you patience if you wait for it."

"I must have patience to be in the business of raising cattle," Carlos remarked.

"But, you have told me that you no longer own the ranch. And, there is something else you have not told me. It might be the reason you decided to come to San Patricio."

Carlos looked at the ground beyond the porch. *How could this old man tell that I had kept a secret from him*?

"I told you about selling the cattle and horses to the Tejano. What I did not say was that my brothers and I plan to steal the steers when they reach three years old, drive them into Mexico and sell them."

"Why do you think this will do you good?" Diego asked.

"The Tejano took our ranch because he must have paid off the judge."

"You speak vengeance. When a man seeks revenge, he can never be satisfied because the hurt remains. You must learn to live outside of the hurt because your revenge on the Tejano will never erase the hurt. You must not be impatient to learn how to live outside of the hurt for which you seek revenge now."

"I am not sure I can agree with that," Carlos said. "The Tejano took everything that we Montoyas worked for."

“What have you been doing since you left the ranch?”

I have worked with my Tío Rugerio at his wagon works in Rinconada. So has my brother, Juan. Pedro stayed on at the ranch because he can tell us what is happening and when they gather the cattle for shipping.”

“Is Pedro happy there?”

“I do not know. He knows what he must do. Juan and I stayed there for a month but left when we had shown the new owner about the ranch and the livestock.”

“You have a year to think about what I have said. If, after your datura is ready, you still seek revenge on the Tejano, you will not be ready for datura because it could be dangerous for you to try.”

“What do you suggest for me while I am waiting patiently for datura to make up its mind?” Carlos asked.

“I see no humor in what you might think funny. Perhaps you can become acquainted with Mescalito and discover if Mescalito will play with you.”

“What exactly do you mean and what is Mescalito?” Carlos asked.

“Mescalito is the name for peyote, but you must not refer to it that way. First we will visit my datura plants. We must walk for a while down the river.”

“When shall we start?”

“I think food would give us strength. Go back to the village. Turn to the right on the big road. Go just outside of the village. You will see an old adobe house with flowers growing in pots hung from the vigas. That is the house of

Hernandez. He keeps goats. Get a young one for birria. I have all the seasoning except onions. Hernandez sells onions, too."

Carlos retrieved the gelding from the corral, mounted and followed Diego's directions to the Hernandez farm where he purchased a young kid and four onions. The entire trip and transaction did not last over half an hour. Diego had already started a fire and filled a kettle half way full of water from his rain barrel. Arriving with the goat under one arm and the onions in his saddlebags, Carlos dismounted and handed his purchases to Diego.

The shaman took a knife from his pocket and slit the kid's throat, catching the blood in a pail. After skinning the carcass, he began cutting the meat away from the bones and tossing it into the kettle. Next came the onions and other spices like cumino, leaves of cilantro and, including, a liberal amount of red chile.

"This feast should be ready by this evening," Diego said. "You picked out a nice chivita."

They sat on the porch as the meal cooked nearby. Diego listened carefully as Carlos explained what had happened to the land that once had been inside the boundary of the Estados Unidos de la Republica Mexicana, but was now inside the boundary of the United States of America. He expressed curiosity about how the new government could take away someone's ranch.

"I understand your feelings," Diego said as he stirred the stew with a wooden spatula. "However, anger will accomplish nothing except to disrupt you from yourself. Anger will not return the ranch to your ownership, if there is such a thing as ownership of land."

"What do you mean, if there is such a thing as ownership?" Carlos asked.

"I live in this old adobe *casa* but do I own it? What happens to it when I am no longer here? Is the ground beneath this casa mine? Does not the earth have any say in the matter of ownership?"

Carlos did not reply, but thought about the shaman's words for several minutes as Diego poured the captured kid's blood into the kettle.

"Think about what happened this way," Diego continued. "The Tejano came in and took the ranch with the permission of someone who thinks he can give permission. The Tejano moves in and uses the ranch for the cows he bought from you. Suppose it does not rain for another year. That will make two years with almost no rain and the year before that there were few rainstorms. The ground is thirsty. The Tejano cannot make the rain. The Tejano cannot tell the ground to grow grass for his cows. He will be angry and his anger will be of no use to him. Avoid anger. Anger is useless to your heart."

"The Tejano will be even more angry because he brought in a thousand Texas steers last year and they have chewed down to nubbins what grass was there."

"So you can see that you have no need to be angry even though you may think you do. Do not be like the Tejano"

When the birria had simmered all afternoon and into the evening, Diego brought a bottle of tequila out of the house and passed it to Carlos. “A little tequila whets the appetite,” Diego said.

Carlos pulled out the cork stopper, took a swallow and passed it back to his host. After several rounds, Diego rose from his chair, went back into the house and returned with two bowls and a stack of corn tortillas wrapped in a thread-bare towel. After handing the tortillas to Carlos, the shaman took a ladle and filled the two bowls with the stew. The afternoon’s cooking had boiled away almost all the water so that what remained took on a richness that Carlos considered a delicacy.

The dog had been sleeping under a mesquite tree with its belly full of the goat entrails. Now that the two men began eating, the dog raised its head to see what else there might be to eat. The smell did not pique his interest, so he flopped his head back down on his paws and returned to his slumber.

After the meal, Carlos took the gelding out of the corral and led him to a stand of sacaton grass by the river, put the hobbles on and took off the halter, allowing the horse to graze throughout the night. A small amount of stream flow persisted in spite of the drought, so the gelding had ample water to drink.

Carlos rolled out his bedroll on the porch and, with his belly full of birria and tequila, went to sleep easily.

The following morning as he sat in the chair sipping coffee, Carlos wondered if Diego planned to speak about datura again. It seemed that the shaman read his thought when he said, “I have decided that it might be best that you not work with datura until you have played with Mescalito. That is, if Mescalito decides to play with you.”

“Can you tell me what this will be like?” Carlos asked. *I thought we were to go to his datura plants once we had eaten.*

“It is impossible for one person to tell another about Mescalito because it will play with you differently than it plays with me.”

He keeps stressing that all this is personal. I am taking grandfather's advice and I hope it is good advice.

Diego brought six grayish green buttons of peyote out of the house. “I have already cut the dangerous white from the top. You must prepare this just as I explain.”

Carlos listened intently to everything the shaman said about how to prepare the plant for ingestion. He followed the directions as closely as he could remember. Diego corrected him twice during the process. It was late afternoon before the shaman declared the substance ready to use.

Carlos grimaced at the bitter taste. Diego handed him the tequila, admonishing him to only wash out his mouth. He began to feel somewhat dizzy and then vomited. Shortly, he thought he could see a bright light that dazzled everything before his eyes.

CHAPTER THREE

He stood on a long plain of grama grass, green and lush, glistening in the sun with the morning's dew. Trains of white thunderheads moved steadily across the azure sky. They were like giant cotton balls because the heat from the plain had not pushed them upward and turn black underneath before spilling their loads of moisture onto the land.

Off in the far distance, Carlos heard a rumbling that came steadily, like a roll of thunder that lasted forever. He wondered what made such a noise because the clouds had not yet broken their trek northward, and there were no shafts of lightning streaking earthward.

He stood in the middle of the plain. Afoot. No horse. No idea where he had come from or where he was going. Just standing. Listening. The rumbling grew louder. He detected a rhythm within the sound. Hoof beats? If the sound were hoof beats it would be from thousands of cattle or horses. Louder. Eyes glued to the direction of the sound, he thought he should see dust if the sound came from hoof beats. No dust. Just the sound of thousands of hooves pounding the earth in a frenzied run.

Suddenly he saw a sea of long horns colored brilliant ebony in the morning sun, flashing here and there. Pure white bodies came relentlessly toward him. He could not run away. His feet were anchored to the ground. He tried to move out of their way but could not. He listened to the sound of the long horns clacking against each other as the white bovine charged toward him.

Their eyes, the color of rubies, stared ahead seeing nothing in their blind fury to reach wherever it was they sought. Their mouths were filled with bloody grama grass blood as they ran. The blood from the grass flew back in thin streams staining the white hair with streaks of red on their sides and flanks. Carlos stood still, resigned that he would be trampled into the ground without a chance to escape. The smell of their sweat was rancid. He tried to run again as the thundering herd drew closer and closer. He could not lift his feet off the ground. Their noses were black where no hair grew.

The herd split as it reached at his position on the plain, taking their deadly long horns with them. The sound stifled until he recognized some famous Texas brands on their hips. The marks were black glyphs on the otherwise white haired bodies of the frantically running steers. He stood still watching, waiting for them to topple and tromp him into the earth. But, the herd kept opening around him as if he were some stout tree in the middle of their path. An island. It seemed like hours that he stood there on the plain. Finally, the herd passed.

He turned around and saw their tails trailing out straight, the tassels at the end full and waving slightly in the currents of air they created. Then they were gone. Disappeared into oblivion. The sound of thousands of hoof beats had ceased. He turned back toward where the herd had come from and saw a plain covered not with the green grassy waving of grama grass in the morning sun, but with greenish wet steer manure. Everywhere he looked was the same. He tried to move from his position on the plain but found he could only turn in a circle. There was no way to leave. The odor of the manure replaced the previous fresh, sweet smell of growing grass. The grass had been trampled into the ground.

Carlos hung his head and began to weep. He watched his tears flow onto the ground, stopped from hitting the surface by the sea of manure that sealed the earth. He wept at the loss of the green grama grass.

Eyes clouded by tears, he looked skyward and saw the thunderheads. They had stopped their northward journey, and underneath they had begun to darken. He kept his eyes skyward so that he would not have to look again at the manure-strewn plain. Some voice within told him that the manure would never fertilize, and only burn what might try to grow. The bastards.

The first bolt of lightning struck close to him, and the brilliance of its fiery light blinded him for moments. The first raindrops pelted down, and he stopped looking skyward to avoid their stinging pain upon his face. He wondered where his horse was. He wanted to ride back home, but he had no idea where home could be. Then he saw that the pelting raindrops were crimson red, and as they struck the earth they turned the green manure surface of the ground black.

As soon as the storm finished dumping, the sun came out from between the clouds that were breaking up and proceeding north or just disappearing, whisping back into the sky.

Carlos stood there in a stupor wanting to leave but unable to move away from where he stood. The sun burned down. The smell of the blackened manure overpowered him. He closed his eyes and covered his face with his hands. *How long do I have left? My lungs will be worthless after breathing the stench of this black cagada.*

Another rumbling. More hoof beats. *Are they turning back because they did not trample me the first time*? Releasing his eyes, he realized that the rumbling came from the same direction as the steers had come. Looking down, he saw that the sun had dried the black manure into a long plain of broken, curling, black crust, like the once muddy silt in an arroyo after the baking sun had robbed all moisture from it.

The noise grew louder as he stood wondering what caused it. A breeze started and began chewing at the curled plaques of blackened manure. He covered his eyes with his hands again. The noise increased and he could hear the staccato of hoof beats, a different rhythm, yet hoof beats. He peeked through his fingers to see if he could discover what charged toward him. Horses. White horses. Thousands of white horses. Each ridden by a faceless man with a white lariat, looped and circling as they came. *Too early to circle the lariat when the cattle have gone. Carry the loop ready over the shoulder. The way you are going your arms will be too tired to throw your loops. Estupidos*!

As the thundering herd of horses came closer, Carlos noticed that the horses were without legs. *How will you catch those steers riding horses that have no legs?*

Estupidos. Dust began to swirl where the horses' hooves should have been. *Why do these legless horses make dust and the sound of hoof beats? The cattle with hooves made sound but no dust.*

As they closed in on him, he again wondered whether they would trample him into the ground. Again, they split as they approached and again he was an island midst the fury. He hoped that none of the circling lariats would, by some error in judgment, fall around his neck and drag him through the now powdery black manure.

As they passed by, Carlos contemplated the legless horses and how they could run across the land. Why legless? How could they be ridden without legs? They were all bridled and saddled. Why? Carlos shook his head in disbelief. The legless horses passed. He looked at their flowing white tails and wondered if they would ever catch the steers, and what would happen if the riders caught them in their loops while using horses without legs. Stupid. With as much brains as a box of rocks.

A dust devil suddenly swooped in and blew the crumbled, powdery black manure into a cloud that disappeared in the distance. Carlos took his hands away from his eyes as the wind ceased, and looked out over the plain. Bare. He turned to look in the direction where the steers and then the riders on legless horses had gone. Nothing. Not a glimpse of either steer or legless horse. He strained to hear the hoof beats. Silence. An ominous silence. He cupped his right ear to try to capture the sound of hoof beats. Silence.

Hearing a swishing sound behind him, he turned back where the bovine and equine invaders had come from. His mouth fell open in wonderment at the sight of a woman dressed in a white transparent robe through which he could see her entire body. His eyes focused on her beautifully shaped breasts with nipples protruding into the fabric.

Lowering his eyes he saw her shapely hips and symmetrical legs that ended in bare feet. Something drew his gaze to her face. He brought his arms up quickly to cover his eyes. Where the robe passed over her head to form a hood, her face showed. But, unlike the rest of her body under the robe her face was not a face at all. It was an empty skull.

"You are surprised, Carlos Montoya?"

He dropped his arms slowly and stood speechless before the woman.

"What were you thinking when you first looked at my body? That is, before you looked at my face."

Carlos stared at the skull as he listened. The bone structure of her jaw with pearly white teeth moved up and down as the woman spoke. It amazed him that her voice came across so clearly. "I do not remember what I was thinking but it must have been how beautiful a body. I have never seen a more beautiful woman."

He continued to gaze at her and watched her smile even though she smiled with bones and not lips.

"You do not always see what you think you see," she said. "You look with hunger in your eyes at my body which you believe you are seeing. Then come to me and put your hands on my breasts. Feel them. Are they soft or firm? Are they smooth and silky?"

Carlos stepped closer to the woman. He reached out with his hands; palms spread out, and cupped them over her breasts. The hard nipples pushed against his palms and he found himself becoming aroused and wondered about the dark triangle he had noticed between her legs.

Glancing at her face he felt his arousal wane. He saw no skull as he put what he wanted in his mind. But, he saw no face either even as he tried to fashion one with his eyes. Attempting to recoup his feelings of lust he reached up to her shoulders, pinched the flimsy fabric of the robe, pulled it around and let it drop to the ground. He stood wide-eyed at the sight of the entire skeleton standing before him. Quickly, he bent down to grab the robe from its rumpled pile at her feet to return it to cover the woman in an attempt to bring back her beautiful, sensuous flesh.

There was a poof! The skeleton disappeared. He stood upright again with no robe in his hands as he looked around to try and see the woman again. He bent over again to grab the robe only to discover that it was being sucked down a tarantula hole in the ground. It vanished just as his fingers were inches away from grasping the flimsy fabric. "You once covered such beauty," he said and began to cry. "When will you return, Lady? Will you return? Or, have you gone forever? Please come back," he pleaded.

He sat on the ground gazing at the tarantula hole.

Hearing more hoof beats, he raised his head, then pushed himself to stand up and look around. The hoof beats came closer but he still could not see what caused them. The sound came much softer than the steers with white hair or the legless horses. The wind blew a dust cloud in front of whatever animals were making the sound of hoof beats. Carlos could not see through the dust. The hoof beats stopped. He felt like they were just in front of him. The dust cloud rolled by and there sitting on two horses, leading one saddled, were Juan and Pedro grinning from ear to ear.

"We are here to drive away the Preston steers," Juan said. "They are all gathered and ready to drive. We came as soon as we could."

"Have you seen them, Pedro?" Carlos asked.

"No. I joined Juan as soon as he came to my place. Do you have a plan?"

"Of course I have a plan. We will dress like Apache warriors and drive the steers away from Toluca at night. Preston will try to follow and we will leave an arrow in a gatepost. When he sees that he will stop following because he is afraid of Apache warriors."

"Where will we take the steers?" Pedro asked.

"We will drive them to Paso del Norte in Chihuahua, cross them over the Río Grande and sell them to Tejanos."

"That is a long drive, brother," Pedro said.

"Better a long drive than to get caught in Rinconada," Carlos said.

"I suppose you know what you are doing," Juan said.

"Where do we get the Apache clothing and bows and arrows?"

"I have them already," Carlos said. "They are hidden in a canyon on the way to Toluca. Let us get started. We need to steal the steers before Preston starts driving them to market them himself."

Carlos took the reins of the extra horse the brother had brought and swung into the saddle. They rode off at a fast trot, Carlos in the lead, heading for the canyon where the Apache clothing waited under a pile of rocks.

With a full moon it was easy to find the cache, and the brothers pulled on the buckskin leggings and shirts. The brightly colored headbands made their black hair resemble the Indians'. They put their own clothing under the rocks and headed for San Ignacio de Toluca at a pace that made sure their horses would not tire before the drive away from the holding pasture began.

Arriving at headquarters, Pedro rode in first to make sure there were no guards to contend with. He returned quickly with the good news that everyone seemed to be asleep in the bunkhouse. Pedro opened the gate to the holding trap. The three Montoyas rode in and began rousting the eight hundred steers from their slumber, without the yelling that usually accompanied such an operation.

The steers that were lying down rose and stretched before heading toward the gate. Others began moving, following the leaders that Pedro had identified previously, and started before the others. A few bellowed softly at being disturbed, but not enough to rouse any of the deeply sleeping cowboys in the bunkhouse.

Surrounding the steers, the brothers patiently eased them through the gate. Juan remained outside to head the herd in the desired direction. Once the last of them had left the holding trap, Carlos took his bow and an arrow and shot it into the gatepost to the holding trap. The false message. Then the three brothers rode to head them south to Mexico without forcing them into a run that might awaken the Preston cowboys or Preston himself.

Carlos kept looking back at the ranch buildings to see if lamps were lit. Finally, he kept his eyes on the herd of stolen steers as they trotted toward the new Mexican border where the United States law officers could not follow the Montoya brothers driving the stolen steers to Chihuahua.

Coming close to the canyon where their clothes rested under the rocks, Carlos rode to the spot, bundled up the clothes, and rode back so that they could change out of the Apache buckskins. Should any Mexican see them dressed as Apache warriors, they would have to defend themselves. He was glad that they had not been forced to look like Apaches raiders at Toluca.

By daylight the drovers had pushed the Preston steers to within ten miles of the new border. By noon the herd walked into Mexico. Carlos continued to check the rear of the herd to see if Preston had sent men to follow the tracks of his steers.

The cattle quenched their thirst in Rio Sonora, north of the former capital, Arispe. Carlos used the time to ride back to a hill overlooking the river and the trail they had taken to the river. At the top of the hill he scanned the western approaches. Satisfied that nobody followed, he returned to the herd as they crossed the river.

For a week, the steers seemed willing to keep moving without much prodding, but when waterholes became scarce they showed some reluctance to leave. At those locations Carlos reminded his brothers "cattle are easy to drive to water but sometimes difficult to get them to leave water".

Hungry days and nights became commonplace for the brothers, especially when they had to spend all their energy to keep the steers moving over the trail to Paso del Norte. On the fifteenth day of the drive, Carlos, who had taken over the "point" or the front of the herd to lead them in the desired direction, saw the hovels on the outskirts of Paso del Norte in the distance. He reined around and spurred his horse to the rear where the brothers rode with bandanas over their noses to ward off the trail dust.

"Paso del Norte is just ahead," Carlos announced, smiling. "We should arrive there by mid afternoon."

"Good," Pedro said without removing his bandana. "After this I hope we can find a buyer for next year's steers closer to home."

"Driving them all this way was worth not having anyone follow us," Carlos said, and returned to his point position.

Where they approached the river it meandered through groves of cottonwood and brushy willow thickets. Glad to see that the banks were not steep, Carlos led the herd toward a bend in the river where there were fewer willow bushes. Looking back, he saw that the steers had begun to hurry after smelling the water. Trotting to the riverbank, he let his horse drink his fill and then began fording the river. Once their thirst became satisfied the cattle would have to be started across. Carlos wanted to test the ford for depth and current before beginning the crossing.

The point of crossing deepened toward the middle of the stream. The cattle would have to swim, but he saw no looming problem with that. Once on the far side they would have only a few miles to travel before reaching Paso del Norte.

Reaching the far bank he booted the gelding up to the flood plain, reined him around and watched as Pedro and Juan kept their places behind the cattle. Carlos hoped that the leaders would see him waiting and begin crossing the river without balking. He cupped his mouth with his hands. “Get them started,” he yelled at his brothers.

Juan and Pedro slapped their reatas against their chaps and yelled at their charges to begin the crossing. The lead steers plunged into the water.

Just then Carlos heard horses approaching him from behind. He glanced back, away from the river and could not believe his eyes. Preston and six men with revolvers in their hands reined up.

"Well, Montoya," Preston said. "Thanks for driving my steers over here to market."

Carlos said nothing.

"Tie this Mex's hands good and tight with rawhide," Preston ordered. Two of the riders dismounted and grabbed Carlos, pulled him to the ground, and lashed his wrists together in seconds, as if they were tying up a calf to brand. As the cowboys pulled Carlos up to his feet, he saw Preston watching the steers begin to swim as they reached the middle of the river. Carlos saw Juan and Pedro rein their horses around and take cover behind some cottonwoods.

The entire herd was now in the river. Before the leaders gained the bank, the river began moving in a strange circular motion. Carlos wondered what was happening when the cattle began being forced into that circular motion. Quickly it became evident that a giant whirlpool had started. It captured the steers in its current and began forcing them under the surface.

"For godsake, what is going on?" Preston exclaimed.

"The river is drowning the cattle," one of the men said. "I have never seen anything like this."

Within minutes the steers had all disappeared. Carlos, wrists still bound with rawhide, looked to see where his brothers had disappeared. He spotted them behind the trees, peeking out watching the crazy happening on the river.

"We might as well take this Mex into town and toss him in jail," Preston said. "Where in hell did that marshal go? He was supposed to meet us here an hour ago."

Just then a man, wearing a star on his leather vest, rode up and joined the group. “Sorry I’m late, Mr. Preston. There was a bit of trouble in one of the cantinas.”

“We caught one of the cattle thieves and the other two are across the river,” Preston said. “I don’t suppose you have jurisdiction over there so I’ll have my men go after them.”

“Mr. Preston, I am afraid I must release this man.”

“What in hell are you talking about, Marshall? He stole my steers and drove them all the way over here. We have been watching them all the way without them seeing us.”

“Mr. Preston, I don’t see any steers,” the marshal said, wrinkling his brow.

“Marshall, I don’t know what the hell happened. We stood here and watched the river turn into a giant whirlpool. It sucked all the steers into it and they disappeared. They were here in the river a few minutes ago. They have to be somewhere.”

“I would think there would be carcasses floating around,” the marshal said.

“I told you the whirlpool was so large it sucked all the steers into it,” Preston insisted. “Maybe they’ll show up downstream.

“Mr. Preston, did you spend the morning in a cantina in town?” the marshal asked.

“Marshall, I think you know that I have been out here watching these cattle thieves arriving with my steers.”

"Well, Mr. Preston, I think you should take that rawhide from the man's wrists. In fact, if you don't, I will."

"Do whatever you want to do, Marshall," Preston said as he swung his horse around and spurred him toward town. The other riders followed him.

The marshal took out a small knife from his pocket and cut the rawhide that bound Carlos's wrists. "There you are, Señor. I would stay away from that Preston fellow if I were you."

"Thank you, Marshall."

The marshal looked out at the river, took his hat off and scratched his head in puzzlement. "I've lived here a good spell, but I've never seen a whirlpool in this river big enough to drown one steer, much less eight hundred."

He put his hat back on and booted his horse into a trot for the ride back to town.

Carlos found himself on the plain again. He sat down on the ground, head in hands thinking about what had happened. He heard a voice.

"Carlos, I am over here."

He raised his head to look in the direction of the voice. "Is that you, Grandfather?"

"Yes."

"Where are you? I cannot see you."

"Your ears must be full of wax. I am sitting over here on my bench. Look to your right."

He turned to his right and there in a haze of some sort of vapor sat Ysidoro Montoya. "Ah, there you are, Grandfather.

I see you now. Your voice seemed like it was coming from inside a barrel."

"Come over and sit with me, Carlos. The bench is comfortable and I have a story to tell you."

"You have told me many stories. Is there a new one?"

"I want to tell you about how my father got the grant for San Ignacio de Toluca."

"What good will that do, Grandfather? A Tejano has robbed us of Toluca."

"I want you to know how the Montoyas came to get it in the first place."

"As you wish, Grandfather."

"As you know, my father, Gregorio Montoya, grew up under the Spaniards. During those times, the King of Spain had gold and silver on his mind. It had taken more money than Spain had in her treasury to force the Moors from España, so when Spain conquered what they called the 'New World', the King of Spain saw a way to retire the Spanish debt from the war against the Moors. Gold. Silver. But that took miners to labor diligently to extract the ore, smelt the precious metal from the ore and then get the booty to the treasury."

"What do you mean, 'booty', Grandfather? Carlos asked.

"It was robbing from the New World to save the Old World. I remember my father calling it 'The King's Fifth'."

"What has all this got to do with Toluca?" Carlos asked.

"You are too impatient, Carlos. Let me free to tell the story I started."

"I am sorry, Grandfather. I will try not to interrupt you again."

"Somehow the Spaniards figured out that they needed to feed the miners to get that ore out of the ground. What better food to feed them than the progeny of the Andalusian cattle that had been exported from Spain to New Spain. So they designed a way. The land grant became the incentive for those who were willing to raise cattle to obtain title to grazing and farming land to be used to feed the miners."

"But, Grandfather, what if those getting the land grants decided not to sell their beef to the mines?"

"Ah, Carlos, the Spaniards knew that the mines were the best market for the products produced by the farmers and ranchers. And, they were correct. You must remember that those in the New World looked to Spain for their government. They were loyal to the King."

"And?"

"After a time they started to call themselves Mexicans. Then, we Mexicans decided that Spain was exploiting us and that we should rebel against what was really slavery called by other names."

"What about San Ignacio de Toluca, Grandfather? Were the Montoyas slaves of España?"

"I suppose in some ways we were. However, those of us who had land grants were not the peons who worked for little or nothing under what they called 'The Hacienda System'. Many of those who owned grants operated them under that system so they too became slave owners in many ways. The Montoyas did most of the work themselves."

"Why would anyone work for nothing?"

"The hacienda owners fed and clothed their workers. Many owners lived in towns and left the day to day management up to their foreman."

"I do not remember any people working for Toluca just for food and clothing."

"There were always enough family members to get the work done without taking on anybody from outside."

"It was always a lot of fun in spite of the hard work when we all joined in the gathers. Now that is over because of that Tejano."

"That is sad, but you must look at it this way. San Ignacio de Toluca did not cost the Montoyas anything. The family made the houses and corrals and dug out the represos for water. We gathered the cattle from the mountains to begin with. Those were wild cattle, but eventually we built a good herd and made a decent living. I am not saying that losing Toluca to the Tejano is all right. But, Carlos, that sort of business when another country comes in and takes over cannot be completely understood by those of us who have lived our lives differently."

"Pedro, Juan and I have plans to steal the steers when the Tejano has them gathered for shipping."

"I cannot agree with that idea. Stealing is stealing in whatever country you live in."

"But, Grandfather, the Tejano stole the ranch from us."

"That is true, but the new law protects the Tejano, not you. Remember, San Ignacio de Toluca did not cost a Montoya a peso. It would not be worth spending your life behind the bars of a jail for attempting revenge. Revenge is a waste of time, and a waste of your life."

Carlos sat on the ground again. His grandfather and the bench had disappeared. Tears flooded his eyes. He wished he could spend much more time with the man who had practically raised him. His tears disappeared, and he stood up to look around.

The rustle of her robe caught his attention. He turned around in a circle and again spotted the beautiful, female figure in the robe approaching him, bare feet on the bare plain. He remembered her and wondered who she might be. She stopped in front of him and held out her hands. Carlos reached out and gave her his and she stroked his index fingers with her thumbs. He had kept his eyes away from her face for fear of seeing her skull. He remained that way as she stroked his fingers gently.

"It is nice to see you again, Carlos Montoya. You are now ready to learn that my name is Lady Truth. I have returned to show you again that what you think you see may not be. Look at my face."

"I am afraid to look at your face, Lady Truth."

"Do not fear. My skull is covered."

Carlos trembled as he attempted to direct his eyes toward where he thought her face would be. She continued to stroke his fingers. He slowly glanced upward. It was not a skull, but it was not what he knew as a face. There was no nose, mouth nor eyes, but there were eyebrows, and ears. He also could make out a chin and cheeks. Her brow, half covered by the hood on the robe, had a smooth covering of what looked like skin, but Carlos was not sure about anything.

"Is this the way you are?" he asked.

"Again, I must say that you do not always see what you think you see."

Carlos stood there before Lady Truth without attempting to remove her robe as he had done before. He could not keep his eyes from concentrating on her beautiful body beneath the transparent robe.

Another voice came out of the darkness. "Ah ha, Montoya, I see this vixen is trying to capture your mind. I am here to tell you to stop listening to what she says. Look at her. She has no face. What you are hungry for you will never have. But I have something for you if you will follow my path instead of hers."

"Who are you?" Carlos asked, and then saw Lady Truth disappear in a small turquoise cloud that rose quickly from the plain.

"I am Lady Temptress. You just saw how easily I sent your friend, Lady Truth up in a cloud of smoke."

"I do not understand what all this is," Carlos said.

"Certainly you do not understand because I have just arrived. I am the only one who can explain all this to you. I am here to show you how to live and still have fun."

"I cannot see you. I do not know where to speak to you," Carlos said.

"You do not need to see me to speak to me, but I can see you and understand you."

"What is it that you have to say to me?"

"Do not to listen to Lady Truth. You will never have fun if you do as she says. She can show you her beautiful body and she can stroke your fingers until you want her completely and then she goes up in a puff of smoke. Have you seen her faces?"

"Yes, I have seen two of her faces."

"How did you like the first one? Is that a pretty skull? How would you like to kiss that face of Lady Truth?"

"Why do you speak this way against Lady Truth?" Carlos asked. "She never mentioned you. She never said anything against you."

"That is because Lady Truth is afraid of me. She knows I can lure you away from her easily."

"How do you plan to lure me away from Lady Truth?"

"Certainly not by stroking your fingers."

Carlos felt hands on his shoulders, kneading and rubbing in alternate movements. He sensed the closeness of something or someone, and came close to reaching out to discover what or who it might be. He remembered when he had reached out and disrobed Lady Truth and the act made her disappear. He kept his arms to his sides.

"You do not respond well," Lady Temptress snarled. "Perhaps next time I will have something that will get you completely. I wish I could use that now and you would never think about Lady Truth again."

"I would like to see Lady Truth again," Carlos said, and listened to the quick swishing movement leaving his presence.

CHAPTER FOUR

Carlos stood alone on the plain. He saw a bright light in the distance. At first it seemed small. Then it grew larger as it eased closer with a slight bounce to its gait. Carlos stared at the light until he felt blinded. He closed his eyes, wondering if whatever approached intended to harm him.

"You may open your eyes now," a voice said.

He recognized Lady Truth's voice. Opening his eyes he saw the back of the robe with the hood over the back of her head or skull, whatever she happened to have under the robe.

"I am glad it is you and not Lady Temptress," Carlos said.

"Thank you, Carlos. I have been hoping you would not fall victim to her evil ways."

"Why are you standing with your back to me?"

"You will discover that in a few moments.

"My grandfather has spoken to me about revenge."

"A wise man, your grandfather, Ysidoro. I hope you remember about the futility of revenge."

"I will try."

"What do you mean you will try?" The voice of Lady Temptress interrupted.

"Why are you here, Lady Temptress?" Carlos asked.

"I am here because I refuse to give up on you. Get rid of Lady Truth and I will show you what I have in mind."

"I am not sure if I want to get rid of Lady Truth."

“If you do not get rid of Lady Truth, I will keep what I have for you and you will never know what it is.”

“But, you are just a voice. Lady Truth is far more than that,” Carlos said. He looked out to see if Lady Truth still stood with her back to him. She had left, but her robe had fallen in a pile on the surface of the plain. “What did you do to Lady Truth?”

“I did nothing to Lady Truth. It was you who made her vanish. She could sense your interest in what I have for you so she left in her disappointment. Now, are you ready for me? Remember, Carlos Montoya, I will do far more than caress your fingers.”

Carlos stood still. He could not deny his curiosity, but neither could he stifle his fear. There was something sinister about Lady Temptress in the way she talked and in the fact that she was just a voice without a visible body. He contemplated his situation deeper. Somehow he knew that Lady Truth would return if he rejected Lady Temptress again. What was there to reject, a voice that tried to lure him into something unknown? But he was interested in what she had to say.

He felt something pushing on his chest. He kept his arms at his sides. The something rubbed around and then stopped. Something tugged at his left ear lobe. Again he stood staunchly straight with his arms at his sides. He could feel a breath on his neck below his ear.

When he saw the buttons on his shirt begin to come out of their buttonholes, he stepped back quickly and buttoned up his shirt again.

"I cannot appear in front of you unless you are naked," the voice of Lady Temptress said. "You must allow me to undress you, Carlos."

He wanted to run away. Where was there to run? She could follow him wherever he ran. He wanted no more of Lady Temptress. He wanted Lady Truth to return.

A crackling noise shattered the silence on the plain. The sound changed to a buzzing that made Carlos cover his ears. His eyes searched for what made the sound, but darkness pervaded. He stood there hoping to see the light approach again. Glad that Lady Temptress had left, he smiled. The buzzing ceased and he let his arms fall to his sides. Far in the distance he saw a small glimmer of a white light. *I hope that is Lady Truth. I want to ask her some things.*

He kept his eyes focused on the light as it made its slow approach as if it felt cautious or reticent. He wondered if the light might bring another thing that he had not yet encountered. Grandfather returning? As he watched, the light suddenly went out as if someone had snuffed it with an upside down barrel.

"Stand just as you are, Carlos," the voice of Lady Truth said, coming from behind him. "I must talk to you for a few moments before I can allow you to turn around. I am continuing from where I left off when Lady Temptress grabbed your attention. I cannot be in your presence when she has piqued your interest."

"I wish she had not been here," Carlos said. "She is strange."

"She is definitely strange and also dangerous. The danger part of her is a thing you may not understand so I will explain."

"I am glad you are back, Lady Truth."

"Lady Temptress has two kinds of power over men. She can tempt you into her fold by teasing you with promises. Once she has you undressed, it would be difficult for you to escape her power. She would then lead you down a path that you might think was pleasure, but that path cannot fulfill, only dig you deeper into her grasp on your mind through your body."

"When you first came into my sight I saw your beautiful body and wanted it. Were you not teasing me then?"

"It might seem that way to you, but I was only showing you beauty."

"But the skull?"

"The skull served to keep you more or less in balance with your emotions. You chose to ignore the skull and tried to disrobe me. That is when I had to disappear. If not, I would have been playing the same role as Lady Temptress. I hope you continue to remember what I first told you about seeing. You do not always see what you think you see. When you turn around to face me, you will be surprised at what you think you see."

"How long must I stay turned away from you?"

"You may turn around now," she said in an almost whisper.

Carlos turned slowly, keeping his eyes looking downward toward the ground. He saw her bare feet and stopped turning. Lifting his eyes slowly upward he looked at her beautiful femininity under her robe. Then his eyes met hers. The most beautiful woman he had ever seen. She smiled. Carlos's mouth gaped open in amazement. He wanted to put his arms around her. He wanted to be next to her. Then he remembered when he had tried to take her robe away.

"Now that you have seen me, Carlos, you can see why Lady Temptress would try to lure you away. Give me your hands."

He extended his hands toward her. She took them in hers and began stroking his fingers as before. He continued looking into her eyes in a complete surrender to her beauty.

"At last, Carlos, you know beauty. Remember when I gave you permission to explore my breasts. Those breasts of mine are beautiful for more reasons than the single fact that you do not possess breasts and therefore find them entrancing. Those breasts are beautiful not only for their part of the female body, but also because they are for nurturing the young. You must also learn that there are other forms of beauty. The beauty inside a person is just as beautiful as the outside and that beauty can be truthfulness, honesty to oneself and others, sincerity of the heart, faithfulness to commitments, and being true to what you believe whether it is from your own originality or from someone else that you may have adopted."

"You seem to have the same type of wisdom possessed by my grandfather, Carlos said.

"I have my own. He has his own. Between the two of us we are trying to enhance your life with an appreciation of life free from greed, revenge and lust without love."

"You have taught me the difference between what Lady Temptress tries to engulf me with and what you insist is a recognition of what is important to happiness. That is the way I must tell you how you have affected me."

"I know that because I have seen and felt where your direction comes from," Lady Truth said. "I now offer you my lips. Should you not accept them in the way you must, which is the way of truth, I will disappear as I did when you attempted to disrobe me. One more thought I send to you. Once you have tasted my lips you might not remember them. However, should you be fortunate and find my lips again, you will recognize them. What you do with that knowledge and recognition is totally in your hands, the ones whose fingers I have caressed."

"Are you giving me permission to kiss you, Lady Truth?"

"Yes, Carlos Montoya, I offer my lips as the love I can give you. There may be a day when you find someone who can give you all her love, and you will recognize the essence of love that I am giving you now."

"Lady Truth, I must confess that I am so in love with you that I doubt very much that any other woman could ever take your place," Carlos murmured, looking toward the ground and seeing her bare feet.

"That is all right, Carlos. I am glad and happy that you are in love with me because that means that you have also listened to what I have said for you. Not, to you, but for you. I look forward to the day when you find and appreciate what you have found with me."

"Here I am standing here telling you that I love you after you have offered me your lips and I am still talking to you instead of kissing you."

"You may have my lips whenever you wish, Carlos."

"I am afraid that should I accept your offer and kiss you, you will disappear as you did when I tried to take your robe away from your body."

"Carlos, I promise that I will not disappear because you kiss me. However, you must understand one thing, and this is the only time I can tell you this. I will disappear, but you might have the opportunity to discover true love. That depends upon your own judgment because I will have been gone from your mind by then."

"Lady Truth, I am very confused. I want your lips. I want your love. But, still I fear that should I put my arms around you, you will be gone in a poof of smoke like you were before."

"Carlos, I suppose I should explain this further. Certainly I am going to leave you. You do not understand that as we stand here facing one another, but you will some day. I do not know when because I am not of your world. Take my lips because my lips are my love to you. My love to you is the love I hope you give to a beautiful lady some day. It is time. Take me in your arms, Carlos Montoya. Kiss me. Let me know that you understand. You can do this with your lips. And, Carlos, remember, if you can, that I love you."

"I love you, too, Lady Truth."

Carlos took Lady Truth into his embrace, looked into her eyes and tenderly found her lips. Slowly, he took her lips with his and held her in the embrace and the moment with his eyes closed in some automatic pulse. It seemed to him that the kiss lasted an hour. He felt a complete ecstasy within his mind.

He stood on the plain, with his arms still in the position of embrace. But, Lady Truth no longer stood in front of him. He dropped his arms to his sides, and searched with his eyes in every direction. He called out to her to no avail; she had gone again just as she said she would. He cried out, pleading for her to return. There was no answer.

CHAPTER FIVE

Carlos could barely open his eyes because the lids stuck together as if they had been glued. He reached up and rubbed the caked stuff away. He could not figure out where he was until Diego said, "Carlos, you are finally awake, no?"

He did not reply. His body felt stiff and sore from lying on the uneven planks of the porch. "How long have I been asleep?"

"You have been there since yesterday evening and it is in the middle of the afternoon now. You must have had a good time with Mescalito?"

Carlos pushed himself up to a sitting position, leaning his back on the wall of the house. "I do not remember anything about Mescalito or what happened."

"You just think you do not remember, but there will be times when you think you have been some place before or known someone before."

"My mouth feels like someone stuffed a cloth into it."

Diego grabbed a bottle from the floor. "Take a swallow of tequila. It will take away the bad feeling in your mouth."

Carlos took the bottle, removed the cork and took a swallow. The burning liquid made him want to spit it out, but he knew the shaman would ridicule him for such behavior. "*Gracias*," he said, and handed back the bottle.

Diego rolled a cigaro in a sheaf of cornhusk, lit it and took a deep drag on his creation. "There is some birria on the stove in the kitchen when you are ready to put something into your stomach."

I know one thing I will never put in my stomach again and that is peyote.

As he became fully awake, he felt something odd on his wrists. He looked down at them and noticed grooves around them like he had been tied up. Grabbing one wrist at a time he rubbed it and it felt better. He repeated the same thing with the other. "Diego, did you have to tie me up by my wrists?"

"No. You did not run around like some do."

This is odd. I wonder what happened. I wish I could remember. Is the old man telling me the truth? He must be. Grandfather had much faith in this man.

He pushed himself up from the floor of the porch, went over to the earthenware *olla* and took the tin cup from its hook. Lifting the cover, he dipped the cup into the urn, filled it and replaced the cover. As he drank, the cool water felt like it was bringing life itself back to his body. The cotton feeling in his mouth had left with the tequila, but the water was the best he had ever tasted. He hung the cup back on its wire hook, stepped over to the empty chair and sat down next to Diego.

"Why is it I cannot remember what happened?" he asked.

"That is one of the mysteries of Mescalito. I do not question it because there is, most likely, good reason for you to forget what happened while Mescalito played with you."

"Now I wonder why take Mescalito if I cannot remember what happened under its spell?"

"This is a question that only you can answer for yourself. However, there have been those who know they have learned to look at matters of the earth differently after playing with Mescalito."

"I will accept that, Don Diego."

"Good. To not accept, you would have wasted the experience. You would have gotten just as much out of pissing up a rope."

Carlos laughed at Diego's humor.

"I think I am ready for birria, Carlos said, and left the porch for the inside of the house where he found the birria simmering in a kettle. He took a bowl from the shelf and ladled in only a small portion to see if his stomach might be ready to be satisfied of its hunger. Hunger or not, the time away from food had played a certain amount of havoc with his stomach. It felt like someone had stirred it with a branch from an ocotillo, spine and all.

Returning to the porch, he sat down again and began to eat. Slowly at first, he spooned small amounts of the rich stew into his mouth, chewing it thoroughly before swallowing. His stomach came back to life. The hunger intensified, and he finished the contents of the bowl in far less time than he first thought he would.

"How do you feel, now?" Diego asked.

"I feel quite calm and now that I have eaten, I feel satisfied that everything is at a proper level and balance.

I have never used those words before, but they are appropriate to the way I feel."

"You are fortunate. That is what everyone expects, but few accomplish. That is exactly the way I feel when I have played with Mescalito."

"How did my grandfather feel?"

"Ysidoro felt the same. He, too, was one of the fortunate ones. I am sure that after playing with Mescalito his life became more in tune with what he had lived before his son, your father, and your mother died from the hands of Apache raiders."

"So he told you about that?"

"Yes. He told me about that in great detail. Your grandfather told me everything that encroached on his mind. He loved you very much."

The two talked into the night about many things. Carlos had surges of emotion when he thought about his grandfather and the shaman. His desire to remember what had happened under the spell of peyote became the only distraction from the conversation. When the moon had climbed high in the sky above them, Diego excused himself and retired. Carlos sat in the chair for a longer time than he knew. Finally, he sensed a feeling on his lips. Rubbing them with the back of his right hand, he suddenly jerked his hand away. "That was wonderful," he whispered aloud. "I wonder what that was."

He slipped from the chair onto his bedroll and fell asleep in less than the time it took for an ocean wave to curl upon a beach.

After they ate breakfast the following morning, Carlos asked Diego why he could not remember anything that happened while he played with Mescalito. "If I do not remember what happened, what is the use of eating that terrible tasting stuff?"

"Some remember, others do not. But it is all in your mind. You might consider it sleeping in your mind. In a year when you return to Datura you might remember what happens then. Some do. Some do not."

Later that morning Diego took Carlos out to the place where his Datura plants grew. After giving Carlos explicit instructions how to prepare his plant, he left him to do it himself, but under supervision. That accomplished, they returned to the house and Carlos gathered his things in preparation for the ride back. With his gelding saddled, Carlos stepped beside Diego. "How much do I owe you?" he asked, knowing that shaman made their livings dealing with such matters.

"You owe nothing. Your grandfather paid for you. He knew you would visit me one day."

"I wish Grandfather still lived."

"We all have our time to live and our time to die. He even outlived his son. That is a difficult thing to live with. It does not follow the order of things, but it does happen."

"Gracias, Diego."

"Go well, Carlos. Be careful with revenge."

"I will do my best."

He mounted the gelding and booted him into a trot toward the village center. The dark eyes looked up from their play, but were glances rather than the stares he saw on his way in. Word passes quickly in small villages. As he cleared the village and crossed the creek that made its way among the cottonwoods, he thought about the ranch and his brothers. He wondered if they would still be taking care of the Toluca cattle when he got back. He would not blame them for quitting if they chose to do so. He had decided on leaving the work on the wagons as soon as possible during his short stay in San Patricio. He felt a need to get on with his life without being tied to the past, or to a job for wages even for his uncle. Montoyas did not work for wages.

He had thought about the various ways he and his brothers could make a living away from the ranch. They all enjoyed working with horses. Carlos could not remember a time when they were without young horses to train. The idea of being dealers in horses and mules in addition to maintaining a livery stable in Rinconada seemed like something to pursue. With the Preston money they had enough to start such a business. At least that is what it seemed to Carlos. *I will talk it over with Juan and Pedro when I get back to Toluca.*

He arrived at the ranch late in the afternoon. He felt tired from the long ride and he realized that he had not fully recovered from the peyote experience. His brothers greeted him with their desire to leave Toluca. They had tired quickly of Preston's autocratic manner and Holt's way of calling them "greasers". They both pleaded with Carlos to leave.

"What about the plan to have one of us work here so we know what is gong on to make stealing the steers easier?" Carlos asked.

"The steers will not be ready to steal for at least a year," Juan said. "I cannot stay here for a year."

"The same goes for me," Pedro said. "We can always ride through to find out when they are gathering."

"I told Preston I would stay until they got acquainted with the ranch," Carlos said.

"Neither of them listen to what we say," Juan said. "Holt thinks he knows everything about everything. The only time he does not say much is when Preston is around. Preston and Holt talked yesterday about bringing in eight hundred steers from Texas."

"There is barely enough feed now for the cows," Carlos said. "That is why I sold the two-year-olds with the threes. Estupidos!"

"I thought they were cattlemen back in Texas," Juan said.

"From what I can gather, they had too many cattle on that range and now it is growing brush. That is why they are all coming over here now that it is the United States and not Mexico. I feel like an orejano without a brand since all that happened."

"I would like to help Tío Rugerio make wagons," Pedro said. "Do you think he would let me?"

"All you can do is ask," Carlos said. "I have been thinking about setting up a business in Rinconada dealing in horses and mules with a livery stable. There are more and more people arriving there from the East. They will need horses and mules and a place to keep their horses and mules when they come to town."

"That sounds like a good idea," Juan said. "I can set up a corner where I can shoe horses and mules."

"I would rather help my uncle," Pedro said.

"Another thing I forgot to tell you," Juan said. "Preston said that since we no longer own the cattle we should move out of this house so he can move in."

"That bastard. There is your excuse to get away from here as soon as you can get packed and find a place in Rinconada," Carlos said.

Packing and moving took longer than any of the brothers anticipated. Instead of two trips to Rinconada, it took six. Instead of one week, it took three. The old house had seen many years as the headquarters of San Ignacio de Toluca. It was the birthplace of the brothers as well as their father. All three had tears rolling down their cheeks when they started the last trip into Rinconada. Leaving the only home they had ever known tugged at their hearts. They rode away without a speck of shame for their tears.

The house they moved into was also old and it took Tía Rosa and several girl cousins the better part of a week to put the place in shape to live in. The house, sandwiched by two other adobes, was the least formidable on Calle Principál. It belonged to a man who had bought it several years before as a rental property, but he had never gotten around to making the necessary repairs to make it livable.

The brothers told him that they would fix things up for a reduction in the rent.

Moving into town proved to be more of an adjustment than they thought it would. Carlos and Juan scoured the area for corrals to rent or even a piece of land where they could build what they needed for their new business. They finally settled on a parcel close to the river that benefited from the shade of tall cottonwoods. There were no corrals of any sort, so they spent a month digging postholes, setting mesquite posts and stacking mesquite logs between the posts in the traditional estacada style. Carlos and Juan spoke often of revenge. Carlos tried to explain to Juan that revenge took up too much of their thoughts and time.

Once the corrals could hold livestock, they went about digging a well for stock water. The water table stood close to the surface with the river so close. Water started seeping into the three-foot diameter hole when they reached forty feet, but they continued digging quickly until they measured the well at fifty feet. They had to hire two other men to keep the water baled out as they dug.

Pedro enjoyed his work on the wagons and every day once they had all reached home for supper, he spoke about what he learned.

The most difficult thing they faced as town dwellers was the close proximity of neighbors. As they reclined in bed readying themselves for sleep, noises nearby made them think that someone was snooping inside the house. Several times they almost bumped into each other as they went to the windows to see what made the noises or to check to see if the doors had been opened. They found life in town totally different than they had been used to at San Ignacio de Toluca, where the only night sounds were coyotes with their yipping chat sessions with one another or owls hooting.

The decision to start a business of buying, selling and renting horses and mules proved to be not only profitable, but also enjoyable. Carlos found breaking green horses more challenging than at the ranch because the horses they bought were strangers. He also liked breaking mules to harness and saddle to give them more value. There were days when his bruised muscles hurt, but he had enough stubbornness in him that nobody could notice he wanted to limp from being bucked off from a particularly feisty gelding and landing in a heap on the ground. The same can be said of Juan, who also proved to be a good salesman. He learned early that sometimes he had to make a customer's mind up for him or her in order to close the deal. He learned to ask, "what name would you like on the bill of sale," which was usually enough to have the client tell him and thereby assure the sale.

Life in the adobe on Calle Principál progressed with the time and effort of Tía Rosa and the cousins she could recruit from time to time. Occasionally she complained of various aches and pains, but never to any great extent. She missed the kitchen at Toluca and the spaciousness of the surroundings. She also missed her garden with fresh vegetables and the fruit trees that provided tree ripened apricots and peaches. Town living did not really agree with Tía Rosa.

She felt too confined. If she had taken walks it might have been easier for her to become acclimated, but her right hip pained her when she spent too much time on her feet.

At the corrals Carlos and Juan built a small barn for feed storage and several horse stalls. It had an attached room that served as a shelter during the daylight hours and a guardhouse after dark with a cot along one wall. They took turns staying there once the corrals filled with horses and mules. They feared Apache raids at night more than anything, but there were also plenty of other horse thieves in the country. They devised an alarm system with thin wire stretched across the gates and bells inside the room that would awaken them at night should there be intruders. They soon began building a tack room for the livery business.

One day when Carlos went to the bank to get money for lumber, Will Barlow asked him why he was improving land that he did not own.

"We thought we owned San Ignacio de Toluca," Carlos answered. "Why should I pay someone money for the land and wake up some morning to find that some Tejano has become too well acquainted with some judge and that I have lost the property?"

"If you continue to rent, Horace Nagle can tell you to leave and you will lose your money and what you have built," Barlow replied.

"At least it will not be land that we have lived on for over a hundred years and it would not be a surprise. Mr. Barlow, you have no idea how it feels to be a Mexican one day and to live on a ranch your great grandfather got from the King of Spain, and then the next day you are a citizen of another country that steals away what you once thought you owned."

"I do not completely understand what happened with Preston and your ranch. Wasn't it something about the papers authorizing the original grant from Spain burning?"

"Those papers burned in Arispe so many years ago I have never even known the date of the fire."

The banker, embarrassed, wanted to change the subject. He wished he had chosen another subject of conversation. "How is the horse and mule business?"

"We are doing quite well for a new business. At least that is what some people have told us."

"That's fine. I am glad to hear that."

"Thank you for referring Walter Jenkins to us. He bought a nice team of mules."

"You are welcome. I do what I can for my customers," Barlow said.

The Montoyas had lived in Rinconada a year and two months when one morning Tía Rosa could not get up from her bed. Carlos had not yet left the office at the corrals when Juan rode up at a lope and told him about Rosa's condition. "Go back and do what you can for her," Carlos said. "I will get the doctor."

Juan returned to the house while Carlos hurried to get the doctor to visit her bedside. After examining Rosa, the doctor left the room to consult with Carlos and Juan.

"Your aunt is quite ill. From her symptoms I can only conclude that she has been sick for some time and probably did not want to worry you. She will need nursing care. I will send a woman who is capable."

"Thank you, Doctor," Carlos said. "What sickness does Tía Rosa have?"

"It is something internal. She is bleeding inside. She may live for a week or a month, but I doubt much longer than a month."

"Tía Rosa has been mother to us for a long time. This is very sad."

Tears filled both Carlos's and Juan's eyes as they stood facing the doctor.

"I will send a woman as soon as I can."

"Thank you, Doctor."

"Incidentally, I understand you deal in horses and mules."

"That is our business," Juan said.

"I would like a good buggy horse that is dependable and strong. There are times when I must keep them going for quite a long time. The horse I have now is getting a bit long in the tooth."

"The next time we get a good one in I will let you know, Doctor," Juan said.

After the doctor left and before they looked in on Rosa, Carlos told Juan about asking Preston for a paper giving the Montoya family access to the cemetery at Toluca. "I have not given it any thought until now," Carlos said. "Preston never gave me that paper and now we will need it. I think I had better ride out there tomorrow."

"If you want to go today, I can handle things here with the nurse and then be at the corrals."

"I think that would be a good thing to do. I do not want to wait until it is too late. I will spend the night out there somewhere."

"If Preston does not give you the paper, what will we do?"

"The cemetery is far enough away from the headquarters that we can go in there at night, dig the grave and do what we have to do before daylight. Nobody will know unless he has dogs that have better ears than the ones we had out there."

Carlos packed his bedroll and enough jerky to eat for two days. He rode his favorite bay gelding out of town heading for the ranch on which he had spent most of his life. This trip was not the way he wanted to return to Toluca. The thought of stealing the three-year-old steers still festered in his mind. He felt that asking for the permission paper was similar to begging since he had made the agreement with Preston. The Texan had either forgotten about it or chose to ignore it. He would miss Tía Rosa. He wanted her to be buried with the family.

Entering the range of Toluca he looked for cattle that he might recognize. Most had scattered from the waterholes by the time he rode past. He noticed some Texas steers that looked gaunt and hungry. Riding close enough to read the brands he saw the T/M to be the newest brand on the left hip of the steers. He wanted to scream after seeing the Montoya brand on Texas steers. It was the ultimate insult. Almost more than he could bear. The bastard.

He saw that the range had been chewed down and the cattle sought what browse they could find on the bushes of mesquite, catclaw and white thorn that still had leaves. What would they do for feed during the cold winter months? Carlos wondered how the neighbors felt about the Tejano Preston and his lust for grass. It was a loss for everyone including the wildlife. The bastard. The changes in the landscape within one year told Carlos Montoya that Steven Preston cared nothing for the land. Carlos remembered what he had overheard in the conversation between Preston and Will Barlow at the bank when he had settled up on the cattle and horse deal. Preston had to be in debt to the bank.

Carlos's grandfather had always impressed on him that he should never let a banker get a hold on Toluca no matter what happened. Carlos mulled this over and wondered how much debt Preston had incurred and what he had promised. His grandfather had said one day that bankers would lend money as long as they were completely assured of repayment either by foreclosure or success on the part of the borrower.

Carlos reached Toluca in late afternoon. He first went to the cemetery. His grandfather's bench no longer stood next to the grave. He glanced around and saw that no weeds had been cut and that the dried stalks of the quelete still stood as guardians of a soil that had been disturbed. He had heard the name "Careless weed" given to the plant that could provide summer feed to native cattle. They seemed to know how much they could eat without bloating. He wondered how many of the Texas imports had gorged on quelites and perished from their greed. Just like their owners.

Stepping into the left stirrup and mounting again, he reined the bay toward the headquarters of the ranch he had grown up on. He trained his eyes on the barnyard and the residence where he had been born, but now he was a visitor. It looked deserted. Nothing stirred. When he got within a hundred yards the dogs finally awakened and came charging out to see who might be the intruder, barking their bluff barks trying to intimidate whoever it might be.

Carlos continued without giving notice to the dogs that kept their distance but continued to defend their territory. He felt strange riding up to the old house where he had been born and lived his life until recently. Reining up at the hitch rail, he dismounted, draped the reins over the pole and loosened the cinch on his saddle. He walked through the open gate into the yard and up the path to the front door. Stepping onto the front porch, he saw the front door open slightly and half of a woman's face peeked out. Carlos stopped. "I am Carlos Montoya," he announced. "I came here to see Señor Preston."

The woman opened the door, no longer hiding behind it. "Señor Preston is not here. Can I help you in any way?"

"I came to get a paper he promised that will give my family permission to continue using the cemetery up on the hill. We lived here for many generations."

She opened the door completely. “Come in, Señor Montoya. Your name is familiar. Señor Preston told me about your family. I am Mary Penrose, Señor Preston’s fiancé.”

Carlos removed his hat and entered the house. She led him into the living room. He was surprised to see that there were only two chairs and a small round table. When they had moved to Rinconada, he and his brothers had almost two wagonloads from this room alone.

“Let me get you some coffee,” Mary said. “Have you eaten supper?”

“Coffee will be fine,” Carlos said as he stared at Mary, watching her every movement.

She disappeared into the kitchen but soon returned with two cups of hot coffee, which she put on the table. “I have put the stew on to warm. I also have some biscuits that I made to go with the stew. You must be hungry after riding here from Rinconada.”

Carlos could not keep his eyes on anything but Mary Penrose. Her fair skin contrasted with her black, almost ebony hair that hung down over her shoulders. Her dark eyes had a sparkle to them that made Carlos wonder if he had seen her before. She sat down in the chair opposite Carlos.

“You are very familiar, Mary. I have a strange and strong feeling that we have met somewhere.”

“Have you ever been to Kerrville, Texas? That is where I have lived all my life until I came out here with Señor Preston.”

“I have no idea where Kerrville, Texas is. In fact, I have never been to Texas. I was born in this house and lived here all my life until your Señor Preston went to the court and took it from us.”

“I do not understand. He told me that he had bought the ranch from the Montoya family.”

“He did not buy anything here except the cattle and the horse herd. That is why I want the paper he promised about the cemetery. My Tía Rosa is very sick and the doctor says she will die soon. I want her to lie in rest in the family cemetery where every Montoya from the ranch has been buried since the time when this country belonged to Spain.”

Mary tilted her head quizzically, but said nothing more about what Preston had told her.

“I do not want to offend you by talking about your betrothed,” Carlos said.

“Do not worry, Señor Montoya. I am glad to listen to you. You see, I may be betrothed to Señor Preston, but I do not know him very well.”

“This I do not understand at all,” Carlos said.

“I would like to tell you about what happened in Kerrville if you will please listen. I have not been able to tell anyone until now. For some reason I trust you, Señor Montoya.”

“Make it Carlos.”

For that matter, please call me María. I will tell you why later.”

“Do you speak Spanish?”

"Yes. I will tell you about that later, too."

"I am sure I have seen you somewhere before."

I am from a ranch near Kerrville. I lived there all my life as you did here. I was sixteen when my mother died. She had been sickly since shortly after she gave birth to me. I am an only child. My father and I buried her at the ranch and then my father took to drink. He missed my mother terribly. That was six years ago. I tried to keep the ranch going in spite of my father's reckless spending in town. He also thought gambling might help him forget his loss. It was not pleasant to watch him kill himself with the bottle."

"Apache raiders killed my parents. My grandfather and Tîa Rosa raised us three boys."

"I first met Señor Preston when he came out to the ranch to try and buy Papa's steers. He offered so little that Papa told him to find some steers elsewhere. Nobody wanted Papa's steers so Señor Preston finally got them for his cheap offer. There was a drought going on and nobody wants cattle during a drought. I have no idea what Señor Preston did with Papa's steers. I only helped gather them."

"Maybe Preston brought them here from Kerrville. I noticed quite a few Texas steers out there on my way here. They sure have eaten the range down. Looks to me like they have eaten all the little rocks and started on the big ones."

"After he came for the steers, he began coming out to the ranch to see me and asked me to marry him. I always said I couldn't marry anyone as long as Papa was alive because I had to take care of him. He got to be a lot of work during his last six months. Not only did I have to cook and care for Papa, I also had to go to town for his bottles of whiskey."

"Did you have any cattle left after he sold the steers?"

"Just a milk cow and she was dry. At least I didn't have a ranch to run as well as everything else."

"It is too bad that your father could not have gone on living after your mother died."

"Yes, very sad. Before he died he lost the ranch to the banker but the banker let us stay on at the house. The banker never put any cattle back on the ranch while we were there. It might still be just sitting there feeding antelopes."

"You must have gone through tough times," Carlos said.

"Yes. Thank you for listening. I have never had anyone I could talk about this to."

"How about Preston? You say you are his fiancé."

"That is something else that bothers me a great deal. Señor Preston came out to the ranch when Papa died. He said that I had refused his marriage proposals before because I had to care for Papa. He maintained that now that he was dead I had no further excuses."

"That seems like putting on the pressure," Carlos said.

"I am not married to him yet and I am wondering a lot about that. He has tried to have me several times and I have always told him that I cannot until I am married. It is the way I believe. Mama told me that before she died."

"I cannot say that I blame him," Carlos said, and smiled. "You are a very beautiful woman, María."

"Thank you, Carlos, but there is more to it than just being beautiful. There are things about him and things he does not know about me that make me think I should not marry him. I know him well enough to know that if he knew I was half Mexican, he would throw me out in an instant. He would throw me out if he thought I was one eighth Mexican. Señor Preston hates Mexicans."

"You do not look Mexican," Carlos said.

My mother was fair skinned with dark eyes and hair. I look just like her. Her family name was Gomez de Durazo. Esmeralda Gomez de Durazo. Papa knew her ancestry but nobody else knew that Merry Penrose was really full-blooded Mexican. After the Battle of the Alamo no one in San Antonio liked Mexicans. And, in Kerrville they did not like Mexicans either. She was only two generations away from Spain. Nobody knows that I am half Mexican, but I am proud of that heritage from my mother."

"I do not understand why you came all the way here if you are not sure about marrying Preston," Carlos said.

"I am petrified of this marriage. I can feel Señor Preston's meanness. I came out here because I had nowhere else to go. The banker in Kerrville said I could stay in the house at the ranch for as long as I needed to. But how am I going to make a living on a ranch with no cattle or horses? I even sold the milk cow."

"I felt the same when Preston grabbed this ranch. It took a while before I could figure out what to do to survive. Now we have a horse and mule trading business besides a livery stable."

"Where is this business?"

"It is in Rinconada down by the river. Go down Washington Street to the end by the river. That is where we are, my brother Juan and I."

"Carlos, I need to ask you a huge favor. Will you help me find a place to stay if I leave here?"

"Certainly. I will do everything in my power to help, including protecting you from Preston if that becomes necessary."

"You have no idea how much I appreciate this, Carlos. Oops, I hear the stew bubbling away. You now must be hungry. I forgot all about supper."

She jumped up from the chair and retreated to the kitchen. A couple of minutes later she came back carrying two bowls with spoons sticking out of them. She put the bowls on the table and returned to the kitchen. The smell of the stew aroused Carlos's hunger. María arrived with a plate of biscuits and sat down.

"It isn't much, but it is better than plain biscuits and water. How is your coffee?"

"I could use a little more. It is good."

She went back for the coffee pot and filled both their cups. Returning to the table and sampling the stew she looked up to see Carlos staring at her again. "Do you still think we have met before?"

"I could almost swear it," Carlos said.

"Can you spend the night? There is a spare room with a cot."

“How about the men in the bunkhouse? They will tell Preston that I spent the night here.”

“There is nobody here. They have all gone to Loping Mule Canyon to try to find the Apaches who stole some horses yesterday. They will not be back for a couple of days according to Señor Holt.”

“Thank you for the invitation. I hope Preston does not decide to come home in the morning,” Carlos said, and laughed. “You might have to leave a whole lot sooner than you are planning.”

“I almost feel like leaving with you in the morning. I know that would not be the right thing to do so I will stay, at least until I can explain some things to him. He will return from Kerrville next week.”

They finished supper and María cleared the table.

“If I am going to spend the night, I need to take care of my horse,” Carlos said.

“It is getting dark, do you want a lantern?”

“I can find my way all right unless they have changed around the grain room.”

He walked to the hitch rail, tightened the cinch, took the reins and mounted the gelding. Booting the gelding into a trot he arrived at the corral in a moment. After unsaddling and putting the horse into an empty corral with a measure of grain and some hay in the feed trough, he walked back to the house.

María met him at the door. She took his hands and began stroking his fingers. He almost jerked them away but decided that it felt nice. “Thank you for listening, Carlos. I am really glad you rode out here today. I feel like I have lifted quite a burden from my shoulders. It is so nice to have a friend.”

“I am glad that I rode out here, too. I am also glad that I have made you a friend, María.” Her stroking his fingers felt familiar. He felt sure that someone else had done the same, but he couldn’t remember whom.

They sat at the table with more coffee as Carlos told her the history of San Ignacio de Toluca and how it became a land grant from the King of Spain. María told him about her mother and the stories she heard when she would sit at her mother’s bedside.

When they finally retired, Carlos had trouble sleeping as he thought about the beautiful girl who slept in the house where he had been born.

CHAPTER SIX

The early morning light obscured the rider heading west on Washington Street toward the Montoya Corrals. It had been Carlos's turn to spend the night on guard in the barn and he had just started taking grain to the horses. He stopped after seeing the rider and tried to distinguish who it might be at such an early hour. He saw that whoever it was wore no hat.

As the rider came closer, he recognized the zebra dun gelding and then saw that the rider was María Penrose. He put the bucket on the ground and walked to meet her at the main gate to the corrals.

"Carlos, I hope that is you," she said.

Carlos looked at her and saw the half closed left eye and the bruise beginning to blacken. Her lip was swollen and she looked about to fall off the zebra dun. "My God, María, what happened to you?"

She reined in the gelding at the hitch rail. Carlos took the reins and wrapped them around the pole. Quickly he went to her and helped her dismount. Once on the ground she put her arms around him. "It was terrible," she said slightly sobbing. "I thought he would kill me."

"Are you talking about Preston?"

"Yes. He came back last night."

"Let me help you into the barn. There's a cot in a room where you can rest. Here, take my arm to steady yourself."

He helped her into the room and over to the cot. Easing her down on it, he stood up again. "I will be right back.

I will take care of your horse and bring you some coffee."

When he returned with the coffee a few minutes later she looked at him with her open eye. "You have no idea what a brute Señor Preston is," she said. "I have never been so afraid of anyone or anything in my life."

"Tell me what happened if you want to. Or, would you rather rest a while?"

"I will tell you in case he has followed me. If he comes here please do not tell him that I am here. I never want to be near that monster again."

"Do not worry, María, you are safe here. If he were to come in here right now I would most likely kill him without thinking twice. Now, let me hear the story."

"I was just finishing cleaning up after my supper when he rode up to the house and came storming in the front door, bellowing like a wounded bull. As soon as he came inside he began calling me a Mex greaser bitch. I knew immediately that he had discovered my secret back in Kerrville but I could not figure out who would have known. It must have been some old timer who knew my mother from her youth."

"What did you do?"

"I suppose I froze there by the sink. I was both surprised and scared. He kept coming toward me and stopped maybe a foot away from me. I could smell whiskey on his breath. Then he told me that he would never marry a Mex. That relieved me even if he did not realize it. He said that I owed him the money it took me to travel here from Kerrville and that I would have to be his maid until the money was paid.

He also informed me that being his maid meant that I would perform other duties. I knew what he meant and cringed at the thought. That is when he hit me in the mouth. He grabbed me by the hair and turned me to face him. He raised his fist to hit me again. I cried out for him to stop, but he struck me just above my left eye. I have no idea what it looks like because I did not wait around after he grabbed my arm and dragged me into the bedroom. I even surprised myself when I kicked between his legs. He yelled out and grabbed himself as he fell onto the bed. I ran out of the bedroom, down the hall and out the door as fast as I could."

"That rotten Tejano cabrón."

"I ran from the house hoping he would stay on the bed. The zebra dun nickered at me when I went to get him from the corral. He must have been disappointed because I did not give him any grain. I had done that earlier anyway. I saddled him as quickly as I could and almost jumped onto his back to get away. I thought about chasing the horse he rode in on away so he would be delayed in case he decided to follow me. I pushed that thought out of my mind because he might have caught me back at the house."

"I take it he stayed on the bed," Carlos said.

"I have no idea. All I know is that he did not follow me, for which I am very glad. If he did follow he did not catch up. He had ridden his horse all the way from here after coming in on the stagecoach and my zebra dun was fresh and eager."

"He looks like he made the trip just fine."

"When I got away from the headquarters so that nobody would hear, I gave him his head for a while. Once I had reached the big arroyo, I slowed him down to a trot."

"That was the Arroyo Garrapata."

"Tick is an odd name for an arroyo."

"I have often thought the same thing."

"Now I am here. I cannot begin to tell you how glad I am that you came out to Toluca a week ago. And, that you told me how to get to this place. I would have had nowhere to go. Thank you, Carlos, for being my friend."

"Well, beautiful lady, I am going to let you rest for a while. My brother, Juan, will be coming in soon and I will send him to get some breakfast for you."

"I doubt if I am very beautiful with this bloodied lip and closed up eye."

"I remember someone saying once that you do not always see what you think you see, but I have seen you before this all happened and I know you are beautiful."

She reached up, grabbed his hand and squeezed it. "I think I will take a short nap."

Arriving for the day's work, Juan found Carlos's story about Maria difficult to understand. "Why would a man punch the woman he wanted to marry?" Juan asked Carlos.

"Preston is about as low as a man can get. María rode all night to get away from him. She must be hungry. If you will go over to García's Cafe and get her some breakfast and bring it here, I will stay finishing the chores in case Preston decided to follow her."

"Why would Preston come here looking for her?"

"He has no reason, but I do not want to take any chances that he could find her. Who knows what he would do to her. Incidentally, Brother, I find Maria quite attractive."

"I can tell that by the way you want to take care of her. I will get her breakfast, but what would she like?"

"I have no idea. Just get something."

Juan mounted his gray gelding and rode east on Washington Street. Carlos returned to feeding the horses, thinking about María and hoping that Preston would stay away from her. He found himself getting angry with the Texan. Angrier than before. Grabbing somebody's ranch was one thing. Beating a woman was unforgivable. *I wonder how he would enjoy a good beating in the cantina at the Hotel Glover some weekend.*

Juan returned with a plate of carne machaca mixed with scrambled eggs. He knew the spicy dish from dried meat with chiles and onions should satisfy her hunger. Carlos walked out of the corrals and met his brother at the hitch rail.

"I will check and see if she is still asleep," Carlos said, and went to the door of the barn that led to the sleeping room. He opened the door quietly and peeked in. Still on her back, María slept soundly. Carlos closed the door and took the plate from Juan. He put it on some shelves by the door and covered it with a flour sack used as a towel.

"I think she needs her sleep more than food at this point. I will give her the plate when she awakens," Carlos said.

"We should see about the gruilla gelding's leg where he cut it yesterday. I will catch him while you get the pine tar."

They got caught up in the day's work. Carlos checked on María every hour. When he opened the door in mid-afternoon, she awakened and sat up on the side of the cot.

"Well, you had a good sleep. I have breakfast for you, but it is almost evening and suppertime."

"I can barely tell if I am asleep or awake," María said. "I am hungry, and I certainly do not mind eating breakfast in the afternoon."

"The eggs have got to be cold along with the carne machaca."

"That sounds like a feast, hot or cold."

"I can ride to the cafe and get you something hot."

"Like I said, a feast hot or cold."

Carlos slipped out the door and into the barn where the plate was still on the shelf covered by the four sacks. He uncovered it and brought it into the room along with a fork. "I will get you some coffee."

Leaving again, he went to get the coffee pot that had remained hot on the coals of the small fire outside. Back in the room he filled her cup, then stood watching her savor the meal in spite of the difficulty she had with her swollen lip.

"So far we have seen nothing of Preston. You must have kicked him hard and with great accuracy," Carlos said when she had finished.

"I have never even thought of such a thing before. I suppose desperation makes you do things out of the ordinary."

"I think you should stay here for a few days until you heal. I would invite you to our house but my Tía Rosa is dying and there are lots of people going in and out every day. It would not be wise to have you there and be seen."

"I am in your hands, Carlos. I have only been in Rinconada twice. Right now and when I came in on the stage from Kerrville with Señor Preston. When we arrived, there was a letter waiting for him at the stage stop. He turned around and went back to Kerrville two days later to make arrangements for a cattle drive. He spent one night at the ranch and tried to have me then. But when I explained about what my mother told me he did not try to force himself on me like he did last night."

"I do not know how long Tía Rosa will last. Yesterday she looked like she was already dead. This is very sad because she is like a mother to us."

"This place will be fine. I already feel better. My head no longer aches where he hit me and I think my lip is less swollen. You are good for me, Carlos Montoya."

Carlos grinned at her as she smiled as best she could with the wounded lip. He took the plate and went outside. Handing it to Juan, he told his brother about his plan to keep María in the room until her wounds healed.

Juan took the plate back to the cafe and returned to the corrals for evening chores. "We need to keep guarding against Apaches and others," Carlos said. "I will bring my bedroll and sleep in the grain room."

"Do you enjoy mice for bed partners?" Juan asked, and grinned.

“Mice in bed are better than Apaches riding away with our horses.”

Carlos rode to the house on Calle Principál, looked in on his aunt before taking his bedroll out to tie on his saddle behind the cantle. Back inside, he helped himself to a serving from a pot of stew and sat down in the kitchen to eat. After finishing what would be his supper, he returned to the corrals and made his bed in the grain room before darkness fell.

María sat on the cot when he opened the door to the room. “Is it dark enough for me to go out and walk around?” she asked.

“In about ten minutes we should be able to leave here without being seen.”

“Good,” she said. “I hope I heal quickly because this room is quite small.”

“I wish I had something better to offer you,” Carlos said.

“It will be fine. I have been thinking about what kind of work I would be good at. Until now the only thing I know is livestock. I ran Daddy’s ranch for six years. Even before that I worked right along side of him.”

“I would say that getting work on a ranch is impossible for a woman,” Carlos said.

“Oh, I know that. It is just that is all I really know how to do. I suppose I could teach school. I read and write both Spanish and English. I am not too bad at arithmetic either.”

“I think you should concentrate on getting your wounds healed. Then you can think about work.”

"I just do not want to be a burden to anyone."

"Listen carefully, María. You are not a burden. You are welcome here for as long as you need to or want to stay."

"You are very kind, Carlos. Is it dark enough to go out for a walk?"

Carlos opened the door and looked outside. Darkness had fallen over Rinconada. "Night is here. We can go out and walk around as long as we do not go into the town."

"Just to get out of that tiny room will be wonderful," she said.

Carlos took her hand and led her away from the corrals, heading north along a trail that paralleled the river. The steady stream gave off a soft murmuring sound different than the gurgles of mountain streams twisting their courses through rocks and stones.

They talked in normal tones without fear of being overheard since most activity in Rinconada after dark occurred in the bars and gambling halls. Carlos, curious about Maria's mother passing herself off as an American, asked the reason.

"After the disaster at the Alamo in San Antonio, Texans hated Mexicans even more than they did before. That defeat shattered their pride because until then they thought themselves invincible. I suppose that is one reason they later defeated Santa Ana."

"Now the Texans come west and bring their hatred with them," Carlos said.

"There have not been enough years gone by for that hatred to disappear," María said.

"I think it is more than hatred. They call us Mexes and greasers and that is more against us as a race. That sort of attitude does not disappear quickly or quietly. It is almost as if they look down their noses at us because there is nobody else to look down on. The same goes with their attitude toward Los Negros.

"At any rate, Mama decided it best to hide our reality as long as we were living near San Antonio, and Kerrville is close."

"You are probably lucky that you have such fair skin," Carlos said.

"I wonder about that. Since I met you the pride I have always felt being Mexican has grown. I hope I never have to say I am gringa again."

"Have you walked enough for one night?" Carlos asked.

"I suppose we had better get back and not leave your corrals alone."

They turned back in the moonlight that picked up the shimmer of the stream as it flowed along through the desert. Carlos put his arm around her waist as they returned to the Montoya corrals. The conversation lapsed as they both walked along silent with their thoughts.

Back at the barn Carlos told her about the bells that served as an alarm system and showed her where he would be sleeping in the grain room should the bells ring during the night and awaken her.

"Good night, María," he said. "It is nice to have you here."

"Thank you, Carlos, it feels good to be where I am not afraid. Good night."

Before sunrise the following morning, when first light made its soft entrance into the valley, Juan came hurriedly into the grain room. Carlos sat up immediately since he was already awake and ready to begin the morning chores. Juan could barely talk through his sobs.

"Tía Rosa died last night, Brother."

Carlos stood up quickly, tears welling into his eyes and put his arms around his younger brother. They sobbed together, patting each other on their backs. "We must go and tell Pedro," Carlos said.

They released one another and Carlos pulled on his clothes. Stopping briefly at the barn room, Carlos knocked on the door.

"Come in," María said.

He opened the door and told her about Rosa and that they were going to tell Pedro. "I will come back as soon as possible with some breakfast."

"Do not worry about breakfast." María said. I saw you make coffee so I will make a fire and start a pot."

Carlos saddled his bay gelding quickly. Both mounted and booted their horses into fast trotting heading for Uncle Rugerio's wagon works. They delivered their message to the rest of the family and stayed long enough to help with the tears. Returning to the house on Calle Principál, Carlos,

Juan and now Pedro entered the house to assess what needed to be done. The woman who had been caring for Rosa told them that she had sent one of the cousins to have the undertaker come and do what had to be done.

The brothers went to Rosa's room and saw her lying peacefully on her back with her eyes closed. Starting with Carlos, each went to the head of the bed, leaned over and kissed her forehead.

"We will always remember our Tía Rosa," Carlos said. "We had two mothers. How lucky we were when most are fortunate to have one mother to care for them."

With everything seemingly taken care of, Carlos and Juan rode to García's cafe and ordered three plates of scrambled eggs and chorizo. Pedro stayed behind to meet the undertaker. Arriving at the barn, they brought the breakfasts into the room where María sat sipping her coffee.

"This must be a very sad day for you," she said. "Please tell me if there is anything at all I can help with."

"I think everything is being taken care of, but I appreciate your kind offer," Carlos said. "Once she has been taken to the undertaker's and all the cousins, other relatives and friends have gone home, you can move to the house. It is best that you plan on moving after dark."

"There is no hurry. I am just glad to be out of sight in case Señor Preston decides to come into town."

Carlos stopped in at the undertaker's to make the necessary arrangements for Rosa's funeral. The relatives living in Rinconada would want to attend, but few would care to go clear out to Toluca for the burial because it required an overnight trip. Carlos, his brothers and his uncle with two cousins made up the burial group. After the funeral, they loaded the casket onto a buckboard, furnished by Rugerio, and drove out to the cemetery at the ranch. They arrived at Garrapata Wash in late afternoon. Deciding to spend the night there instead of near the ranch headquarters, they made their camp ate supper and hobbled the saddle horses. At dusk they rolled out their bedrolls, hoping to get a good night's sleep prior to the difficult chore of digging Rosa's grave in the morning.

Arising early, they ate breakfast, prepared by Rugerio, and arrived at the cemetery just as the sun peeked over the Sierra Cimarrón. They carried a pick, crowbar and two shovels in the buckboard. Taking turns, they dug the grave through the rocky ground.

They put two short logs in the bottom of the grave and, with two ropes under the casket, lowered it into the grave. Once it rested on the logs they pulled the ropes out and began shoveling in the dirt, burying the casket. They were piling rocks on top of the grave to discourage coyotes and other scavengers from digging when Preston and Holt rode up from the ranch headquarters.

"What in hell goes on here, Montoya?" Preston demanded.

"We have just finished burying my Tía Rosa," Carlos said, leaning on a shovel.

"I don't want no more Mexes in this cemetery," Preston said.

"When I sold the cattle and horses to you, we had an agreement about this cemetery. You promised to give me a paper giving permission. You seem to have forgotten."

"I haven't forgotten a damn thing, Montoya. I decided I didn't want no more Mexicans here."

"You also seem to have forgotten that we are Americans since your Mr. Gadsden bought this land from Mexico."

"Montoya, you are trespassing. You had better get off my land or I'll have the sheriff put your greaser ass in his American jail."

"We will be finished in a few minutes, Preston. We would appreciate it if you would leave while we pray for our Tía Rosa."

"Just don't bring any more of your people out here to bury," Preston said, and the two reined their horses around and left the cemetery.

Carlos asked the family group to bow their heads, and he said what words he could wishing Rosa well in her new life. Then they gathered the tools, loaded the buckboard, and made the trip back to Rinconada, arriving just after dark.

Carlos put up his horse and went to the room in the barn where he hoped to find María. She had come to the door before he arrived. "That must have been a sad trip for you," she said.

"Yes. And, Preston rode up just as we were finishing the burial. He is really full of hatred."

"Did he ask about me?"

"He doesn't seem to connect you with me. He just reneged on his permission for my family to continue using the cemetery. I think it is a good time for you to move into our house on Calle Principál. This room is far too small to live in."

"I am ready," María said.

Darkness hid them from view. Once inside, Carlos showed her the room where Tía Rosa had slept. "You may have this room unless it bothers you that Tía Rosa died here," Carlos said.

"This is fine. That does not bother me."

"I will see you in the morning. It is my turn to stand guard at the corrals."

Carlos left for the corrals, and spent the night in the room once he had seen that all was well in the barn and stall area. The trip to Toluca had tired him. As he fell asleep he recalled the many years his aunt had been with him and his brothers. He soon fell into a deep sleep and awakened after the sun had risen. Groggily, he set out to do the morning chores, hoping that Juan would show up soon to take over while he went back to the house to see María. He realized that while he was away at Toluca, he had missed talking with her.

When his brother finally arrived, Carlos rode back to the house, put his bay gelding in the corral in back and went in to see María. She stood in front of the stove cooking something. As he walked in she looked up and smiled. "I knew you would be here soon, so I started breakfast. Juan had his before he left."

"That sounds like something I will enjoy. Have you had yours?"

"Not yet," she said. "I thought it would be nice to eat with you now that I am all settled in here. It is certainly more comfortable than that little room."

"The room served its purpose. Nobody has seen you in the company of the Montoyas. You cannot tell what a man like Preston would do if he knew where you had gone."

"I am sure you are right," she said, and began putting the meal on the plates she had kept warm in the compartment over the stove. Carlos sat down when she put the plates on the table and brought the coffee pot over to fill the cups. Placing the pot back on the stove, she sat down.

"Thank you for the breakfast," Carlos said.

"You are more than welcome, Carlos. I can never repay you for your kindness."

"Your smile is plenty."

Carlos told her about Preston at the cemetery and how they continued with the burial in spite of his presence. "I must say that I missed you while I was gone," he said.

"I missed you, too," she said, and paused. "There is something I need to ask you. When I ran away from Señor Preston, I left a few things in my room there. The clothes I brought from Kerrville are not as important as a small wooden box that contains a cameo that my mother gave me and two hundred dollars that I also put into it. The box is hidden behind the top drawer of the dresser in the room where I stayed. Will you help me get my things, especially the wooden box?"

"I will certainly help. Getting into that ranch house might be difficult and of course risky, but let me think of a plan. It cannot be impossible."

"I will appreciate your help, Carlos. The money will help me to not feel like a burden."

"Dear María, please stop thinking that way. You are not in any way a burden," he said, and reached for her hand.

CHAPTER SEVEN

Maria's request weighed heavily on Carlos's mind. He wanted to help in any way he could, and getting her things away from Preston would certainly be satisfying. What bothered Carlos was the risk of getting caught in an act that could be construed as burglary even though she would be there to get what belonged to her.

After thinking for close to two days, Carlos stayed at the table after breakfast to discuss a plan that he hoped was not too risky.

"I have talked with Juan about Preston," Carlos said. "Juan has mentioned seeing Preston in town. He thinks that Preston comes to town on Friday afternoons. He drives a buckboard to haul supplies back to the ranch. He stays at the Glover Hotel and Juan has seen him drinking enough whiskey to make him talk loudly at the bar in the Glover."

"How long does he stay in town?" María asked.

"Juan said that Preston often stays at the Glover until Sunday morning, but sometimes he has seen him leave around noon on Saturday."

"It is too bad that he is not more consistent," María said.

"It would certainly make our planning easier. I think what we need to do is scout the Glover to see when he arrives on a Friday. Once he is there we can be reasonably sure that he will spend the night in order to get ranch supplies Saturday morning. I also think he enjoys a night at the Glover bar."

"This sounds like we must make sure he will spend the night," María said.

"It would be easier if he kept his buckboard at our livery, but I have never seen him there. He probably thinks we will steal his team. I hesitate to ask anyone at the Glover what his weekend plans are, because they might tell Preston that Carlos Montoya is asking questions. One never knows."

"I understand what you mean. We must outguess him, or we run the risk of him discovering us should he return early to the ranch," María said.

"That just about sums it all up. However, if we can scout the Glover on a Friday afternoon and follow him to see where he keeps the buckboard, we will know if he intends to spend the night. If the team gets put up for the night at the other livery stable, we should be able to get out to Toluca and back with your things by the following morning if we leave as soon as we see what the situation is."

"You have thought a lot about this," María said.

"I have had little on my mind except this since you asked me to help you retrieve what is yours from Toluca."

"Again, I must thank you for your kindness," she said.

"Today is Thursday. Tomorrow I will have Juan scout the Glover since Preston has probably seen him there before. He can follow Preston to the other livery and see what arrangements may have been made. As soon as he has done that, he can ride here to tell us what he has seen. Then he can go back to the bar at the Glover Hotel, see if Preston is drinking, and get back here to tell us. We will be ready with our saddle horses to ride for Toluca. Can we get everything you want on saddle horses, or do we need a pack horse as well?"

"What I want most is the box with the cameo and money. If I can find room behind our saddles for a few clothes that will be extra. If we do not have time for clothes I will gladly leave them there."

"I do not think we should take a pack horse, in case we have to make a run for it should Holt or the cowboys discover us. Or, for that matter, if Preston decides to come home early."

"Preston may have thrown all my clothes out by now. After all they warmed the body of a Mexican."

"I have been meaning to ask you if you want to get some clothes here in town. All you have is what you wore in."

"I have been able to wash these, and if I can get some of the clothes I brought from Kerrville, I will be fine. Lots of women would be crazy wearing one set for as long as I have, but I am a ranch woman. I can manage my life with far less than a city woman."

"You are a very special woman, María," Carlos said looking into her eyes. She smiled and looked away.

"I suppose I had best get down to the corrals and give Juan a hand at whatever needs to be done today."

On Friday afternoon, the clouds that had hidden the mountains all day lifted away from the land and the sky became clear and blue. Juan left the Montoya corrals at four o'clock and headed for the Glover Hotel to see if Preston had decided to come to town for the weekend. Carlos started doing the evening chores, feeding the zebra dun and his bay gelding first in case they needed to head to Toluca. He had just finished the feeding when Juan arrived in a state of exhilaration.

"What did you find out?" Carlos asked as Juan rode up and jumped from his gray.

"He came to town all right and is playing poker and drinking in the Hotel Glover bar. I watched him arrive driving his buckboard with a saddle horse tied on behind. He must be figuring to do some visiting," Juan said, and laughed.

"Then it looks to you like he is here for the night?" Carlos asked.

"The buckboard and team are at the Hungerford Livery and his saddle horse is tied to the hitch rail at the Glover. Maybe he has a girl friend."

"More than likely he has his saddle horse there so he can ride to the houses over on the shady side of town once he gets tired of the poker game."

"You are probably right. What do you want me to do now?" Juan asked.

"Keep watching him at the Glover. I am going to saddle Maria's zebra dun and my bay. If I do not see you by the time we are ready to go, I will assume that all is well."

"I hope I do not have to stay there at the Glover too long."

"Once he goes to his room you can quit watching him. If he goes over to the whores, you might as well quit watching him, too."

"All right," Juan said. "Good luck at the Toluca. If you ride near the cemetery, give Grandfather and Tía Rosa salutes from me."

"I will do that. And thank you for the help."

Juan mounted his gray gelding and started back to the Glover Hotel. Carlos saddled the bay and the zebra dun, and rode to the house on Calle Principál. María came to the door as he arrived. "I see you have the dun saddled. I gather that Señor Preston is in town and we are headed for your ranch," she said.

"You are right. Juan is watching him at the Glover. He has a saddle horse tied to the hitch rail, but we both think he might be thinking about going to the ladies of the night."

"I feel sorry for them."

"We need to get going," Carlos said. "It is a long ride and we need to save our horses for the ride back. It should be dark within three hours, but the moon is almost full so we will have light to travel by."

"I am as ready as I can be," María said. "I made some carne seca and wrapped it in tortillas for us to eat when we get hungry."

"You think of everything," Carlos said.

They left the house, mounted their horses and Carlos led the way out of town skirting the area of most activity. Once beyond the town and on the road that led to the ranch and beyond, Carlos reined up and explained what Juan had observed and that they were lucky to have Juan to scout Preston. Also, he told her the need to save their horses as much as possible for the ride back when speed might be the factor between getting caught and getting away with what they had gone for.

They rode with their own thoughts for an hour. Carlos thought about the trip to recover Maria's few possessions. He knew that returning to Toluca would be as difficult for him now as it had been when he first met María and then later when they had buried Tía Rosa. He wondered if his anger at feeling robbed of the family land would ever fade. Going to Toluca had not been easy, but meeting María had been one of the happiest times he had enjoyed in recent years. He tried to remember who she reminded him of and why the way she stroked his fingers seemed so familiar. He wondered what it would be like to make love to her naked.

"This is a beautiful trail," María said, breaking the silence between them.

"I like the cottonwoods by the river and the mountain boundaries of the valley," Carlos said. "This is where I was born, but now that it is no longer Mexico, I often wonder if it will be where I die. I once thought that I would spend my life in this beautiful valley."

"You will have a very long time to think about that, Carlos," she said and smiled at him.

"I know that, but the Montoyas called this valley home for so many years and now I can no longer live on the old

San Ignacio de Toluca. What is this Gadsden Purchase that made me other than a Mexican citizen just because someone wants to build a railroad?"

"I do not know all about that. Back in Kerrville, we were Mexicans and then we were Texicans and then we were called greasers. It was all confusing. My mother and I were lucky that our skin is fair like the gringos. But that has its disadvantages, too. One loses his or her identity as a Mexican."

"That is exactly what happened to me. I even lost the family ranch. I am not sure what will happen with all this change. I have even thought about going to live in Sonora."

"But what would you do there to make a living?" she asked.

"I do not worry about making a living. I know livestock. I know how to manage. Making a living is the least of my worries."

"What do you worry about, Carlos Montoya?"

"I suppose I worry about getting your things back from the ranch.I do not worry about much. I have learned that worry makes your stomach tighten like it was bound in drying rawhide."

"Do you worry about me?" María asked.

"No, I do not worry about you because I know you can take care of yourself."

"But, I am a woman. Does that not concern you?"

"You are quite a different kind of woman than I have ever met."

"Have you known a lot of women, Carlos Montoya?" she asked with a smile and a twinkle in her eye.

"Fewer than most my age. I spent most of my time at the ranch."

"You have told me that Señor Preston took your ranch. I do not understand how he did that," María said.

"I am not completely sure how he managed to get the ranch away from us, but I have some ideas. After the Gadsden Purchase, this part of Mexico became part of the United States. When it was Mexico, Mexican customs prevailed. One was *mordida*, the bite or bribe. I am sure you know about that in Texas," Carlos said.

"I suppose any place that was once part of Mexico has heard about mordida, "María said.

"We used to accept that to get anything done through the government we had to pay the government officials a bribe, mainly because the government salaries are too low. But, those bribes were known and were above the table. No surprises."

"I never got into that part of the business. Our ranch had been established before I began running it."

"You are lucky, because it is no different in the United States except here it is done under the table. That is what I think happened in the matter of San Ignacio de Toluca and Preston. There had to be some judge friendly to Preston for a reason, and the reason was most likely money."

"Are you certain about this?"

"Not really, but I do not see any other way it could have happened."

"Did you fight the situation?"

"I am not experienced in that sort of thing and we have very little cash to pay some lawyer. Besides, I do not trust a lawyer to represent us against a Tejano cattleman and a former Tejano who is the judge."

"I think I understand things better now that you explain about bribery. It seems too bad that honesty does not matter to many."

"Lots of people have no idea what honesty includes," Carlos said. "Those who stoop to bribery often think it is acceptable."

They rode along in silence for a while. The trail passed through a mesquite bosque that bordered the main river channel through the valley. Every so often the groves of mesquite gave way to stands of lofty cottonwoods whose leaves rustled in the night breeze. The river carried very little water because of the drought that had become a scourge to those raising cattle, horses and sheep.

They stopped about half way to Toluca and let the horses drink from the meager stream. "Are you hungry?" María asked.

"Not yet," Carlos replied. "We need to push on and get there as soon as we can without using up the horses."

"This river is beautiful in the moonlight," María said.

"It is more beautiful with a normal amount of water in it."

With their heads lowered, the horses began to drink from the stream. Carlos and María were close to one another. Out of the corner of his eye, Carlos saw a movement downriver. He glanced at it and saw a cougar cautiously approach the stream. It had looked around after coming from the tall sacaton grass that grew on the river's floodplain. But, with the two riders and their horses downwind, the big feline continued without alarm.

Carlos reached over and touched Maria's arm, and put his finger to his lips to tell her to be quiet. Then he pointed to the beautiful tawny colored cougar at the water's edge quenching its thirst, slurping the water with its tongue. Carlos grabbed the stock of his carbine in its scabbard, began lifting it slowly out, and then abruptly stopped and let the rifle slip silently back where it had come from.

Just then the horses lifted their heads from the stream and looked at the cougar. They snorted almost in unison and the cougar whipped around and dashed into the sacaton grass, disappearing in an instant.

"What a beautiful cimarrón," María said.

"If the horses had not picked up its scent, it would still be drinking."

"You started to take out your carbine to shoot it. What made you change your mind?" María asked.

"I am not sure. I used to kill them because they killed my cattle and horses. Now, I don't need to kill them.

They reined the horses away from the river and trotted back to the trail. Carlos rode in silence, thinking about the beautiful cougar drinking at the river's edge.

As they rode along keeping a steady pace, they looked at one another occasionally and smiled. Crossing the Arroyo Garrapata, Carlos looked to the eastern horizon to see if early morning light had begun to show itself. "We are almost there," he said.

"I have been thinking about this. I am putting you in danger just wanting a cameo and some money. Perhaps we should turn back and forget about my whims."

"You are in the same danger as I am. This is something that we must do together. Preston stole my ranch, so I am making sure he doesn't get your cameo and money. It is far better that I am with you in this adventure than for you to try it alone."

"I hope we are successful and do not get caught by any of the ranch people."

"If we are careful, we will ride in from behind the hill to the house and nobody from the bunkhouse will see us. By the way, I have some raw beef in my saddlebags. If their dogs come out to meet us, I will toss them the treat to keep them occupied and to make them think they are among friends."

"You seem to have thought of everything, Carlos. I completely forgot about those dogs."

"I am wondering if Preston has put locks on the doors. Do you remember?"

"I never noticed any locks," María said.

"We never had any locks because there was always someone around to take care of the place. The Apache raiders who killed my parents and sister were the only ones that locks might have delayed, and I am sure not for long."

"Are the Apache still raiding?"

"Sometimes. The American Army tries to keep them away from settlements, but they appear at times. It is almost like they arrive to shop for provisions. I have thought a lot about those raiders. Before the Americans came the Mexicans faced the problem of the Apache. Before the Spaniards came here from the south, the Apache considered all this land their territory. But, the Spaniards brought them guns and horses. It is almost the same as when the Americans bought this land from Mexico and we became American citizens, whether we wanted to or not. That is, if we wanted to stay in our homes."

"I have also been thinking about these things," María said. "You and I have both been raised on ranches and now we have lost those ranches. We certainly have a lot in common."

Carlos looked over at her and smiled. María did not turn her head because she saw the Toluca headquarters in the moonlight. "We are here, Carlos."

"I know. Now we have to be quiet and ride around that hill away from the bunkhouse. It should be light soon and I want to be out of here by then. Once we reach the house, I will go in first. You wait outside. When I see that there is nobody inside, I will come back and get you. Then we go to your room and get the things we came for. If the dogs come right away, I will give them the meat. If they are not at the house, I will give you the meat in case they arrive while I am inside."

"I hope this turns out all right."

"It will. If anyone comes snooping around while I am inside, take the carbine from the scabbard and point it right at their belt buckle, then give me a yell."

"Hopefully, nobody will come snooping around."

They rode a large circle around the headquarters so that they would approach the ranch house out of sight of the bunkhouse where the men slept. Carlos hoped that they did not arise too early and somehow discover him and María. Fifty yards from the house, Carlos reined in and dismounted, motioning for María to do the same. Slowly and as quietly as possible they led their horses to the hitch rail in front of the the old adobe house where Carlos had been born. After wrapping the reins around the pole, Carlos reached into his saddlebags and brought out two packages of meat and handed them to María without saying a word.

Carefully he stepped up to the porch and went to the front door. Turning the doorknob so the latch would not make a sound, he opened the door and stepped inside. Tiptoeing down the hall, he looked into the rooms to make sure they remained empty in Preston's absence. After reaching the kitchen, he turned around and headed back to the entrance, satisfied that the house stood alone.

He beckoned María to come in. She held out the packages of meat to question what she should do with them. Carlos motioned back to toss them on the ground in case the dogs arrived while the two of them were inside. She tossed the packages at the base of the porch steps and followed Carlos inside. He waited by the door and closed it. He had found a lantern on a small table by the door, just where the Montoyas had kept one. He lit it and turned down the wick. María led him to the room where she had stayed.

Once inside, she lost no time in taking the top drawer out of the dresser as Carlos held the lantern for her to see what she was doing. The wooden box was still there held on by a strip of cloth tacked to the back of the drawer. María took it off by twisting the box and ripping the cloth strip. She handed it to Carlos, who stuffed it into the pocket of his denims. Stepping to the armoire, she opened the door and grabbed the clothes that were on hangers. Looking at a pair of shoes, she dismissed the idea of taking them.

"I have everything I need," she whispered.

"Then we should get out of here as quickly as we can."

As they approached the front door, Carlos saw him first, standing, blocking their escape. Carlos stopped and María nearly walked into him.

"Well, Montoya, what are doing here with that goddamn Mex bitch?" Preston said, pointing his forty-four at them. "I ought to kill you both right here and now. You are both trespassing."

"We are here only to get Maria's clothes, Preston."

"She could have taken them with her. Since she didn't, I figure those clothes belong to me since they were left in my house," Preston said, emphasizing "my". "I am glad you rode the zebra dun tonight, Mary, María, because he is back where he belongs."

"You gave me the zebra dun, Señor Preston."

"That was a wedding present, but there was no wedding. Now I have to figure out what to do with both of you since you have burglarized my house."

"Preston," Carlos said. "Why not go about your business, whatever it is, and we will ride back to town with Maria's clothes?"

"No, Montoya. No goddamn Mexes are going to get away with burglary. You two are going to walk in front of me over to the bunkhouse where I will get my men to tie you both with rawhide to your saddles. Then I'll take you to the sheriff."

Just as Preston opened the door to lead Carlos and María outside, a stern voice spoke. "Preston, drop that gun and raise your hands as high as you can, or you are a dead man."

Preston dropped the revolver on the floor and raised his hands.

"Juan, how did you get here, and just in time?" Carlos asked.

"I will tell you the whole story on the way back to town. Right now, I want to make sure this Tejano cabrón comes to understand us."

Juan moved around to face Preston, kicking the revolver away as he did. "Preston, if you try to set the sheriff on my brother or María, we will be witnesses to how you beat her up before she rode into town. And, furthermore, you will not live to go into court. I will guarantee that. You are one lone Tejano in the midst of a lot of Montoyas, any one of whom would be happy to see you become buzzard bait. Do you understand what I am saying?"

"I understand you, Juan. Now I know why you were in the Glover bar last night."

"That is the first time you have shown any intelligence. Carlos, get that forty-four. We will leave it at the Glover. You can pick it up when you return to your losing poker game," Juan said. "Another thing you should think about is if we were here to rob you, we would take your money right now. I know you went broke at the poker table and came home for more money.

Carlos stepped over, picked the gun up from the floor, and shoved it behind his belt. "Preston, we are also taking your saddle horse with us, but we will turn him loose at the Garrapata," Carlos said. "He should be able to find his way home. Now, it is time for you to get inside and close the door. We will be on our way."

Carlos took Maria's clothes, divided them into two bunches, and tied them behind the saddles. With Juan leading Preston's gelding, the three mounted and they booted their horses into fast trots away from the Toluca headquarters. Carlos looked back, but saw no sign of

Preston. At the Garrapata, they knotted Preston's reins around the saddle horn and turned the horse loose.

"Are you men hungry yet?" María asked, before they started out again.

"I can eat something," Carlos said.

"I could eat a rotten javelina," Juan said.

María took the wrapped dried beef from her saddlebags and handed it to the two brothers. She unwrapped another and began to eat.

"While we are stopped here, Juan, tell us about the poker game at the Glover Hotel bar," Carlos said.

"The poker game was comical," Juan began. "It was not funny to Preston because he could not win a single hand. Either someone at the table brought in a stacked deck or the Tejano had no decent cards dealt him. I stayed there like we planned. It was not too long before they broke him. He had had plenty to drink, so he told them to hold his place until he rode home for more money."

"They must have laughed if they knew how far he had to ride to replenish his money," Carlos said.

"Nobody laughed. As far as I know they kept on playing without Preston. I left shortly after he did and saw that his horse was not at the hitch rail. I got going and saw him ahead of me. I reined in and let him get a good lead so he would not see me if he turned around in his saddle."

"How soon after we left did Preston leave the bar?" Carlos asked.

"Maybe twenty minutes," Juan said. "I just hoped he would not hurry too much and catch up with you and María. As it turned out he never knew you were ahead of him. I made sure I was close behind him as he rode into headquarters. I would say that I timed it rather well."

"You could not have timed it better," María said. "If you had not shown up when you did there is no telling what he would have done."

"We should not waste any more time in case he decides to ride after us or get back to his losing poker game." Carlos said.

They finished the carne seca wrapped in tortillas and continued on the trail into Rinconada. From time to time, Carlos glanced back over the trail to see if Preston followed, but there was no sign of him all the way to Rinconada.

Before riding back to the corrals, they stopped at the house on Calle Principál to allow María to put her clothes inside. Then they rode to the corrals and put up the horses. Juan stayed to guard against Apache raiders and Carlos accompanied María back to the house. She immediately set about cooking a meal. Carlos put Preston's forty-four on the kitchen table. Then he took the wooden box from his pocket and handed it to María. "Here is what we went to rescue," He said.

"Thank you again, Carlos. This means a great deal to me since it is all I have with which to remember my mother." She opened the box, took out twenty dollars and handed it to Carlos. "Take this to help pay for my keep," she said.

"Keep it in the box," he said. "I will tell you if I need any money for your keep."

She refused to put the money back into the box and stood there glaring at Carlos. "I intend to pay my own way, Carlos. You have been more than kind to me by taking me in and protecting me against Señor Preston. I do not want to be any sort of burden. Why don't

"Perhaps I want to take care of you," he said.

"You may not be seeing in me what you think you see," she said.

Carlos scowled, wrinkling his brow. "There it is again. I have heard that before but I cannot remember where or from whom."

"Well, it is true. I am not a weak dependent woman who needs to be taken care of. You must remember that I ran my father's ranch for several years."

"I must say, you do have a stubborn streak," he said.

"Call it anything you want to, but I am me," she said, and smiled at him.

"María, you are different, that is certain. And, I like that."

Carlos stepped toward her and took her into his arms. He could no longer resist her lips and kissed her. María returned his passion with hers. As their lips parted, Carlos became suddenly pensive and looked beyond her eyes. "I have kissed those lips before," he said.

Without releasing each other, they stood in the middle of the kitchen. "You have never kissed my lips before, Señor Montoya. You must have been dreaming."

"That is a possibility. There is a lot about you, María that seems familiar. I know I have never felt the same feelings with any other woman even though I have not known many women. I have been trying to figure out what these feelings mean. The only thing I can think of is how much I love you."

"I love you, too, Carlos Montoya. You are the first man I have ever loved."

Carlos took her head in his hands and kissed her again with even more passion than before. When they released one another, they were breathing rapidly.

"It might be a good idea for us to go for a walk," María said.

"I had something different than a walk in mind," Carlos countered.

"That is obvious," she said, and broke away from their embrace. "Why not take Señor Preston's gun to the Glover Hotel. Supper will be ready by the time you return."

"Are you teasing me, María?"

"I have no idea what you are talking about," she said. "I only know that we need to have caution right now."

"Why?" he asked

"I have already told you about what my mother told me. I intend to follow her good advice."

"I suppose this means we must get married," Carlos said.

"No. My mother only said that I must maintain my virginity until I am married. This is really becoming embarrassing to me, Carlos. Is it too much to ask that we change the subject of this conversation?"

"I will take Preston's forty-four to the Glover," Carlos said, and smiled.

CHAPTER EIGHT

After breakfast the following morning, Carlos and Juan were at the corrals. An army officer rode up and dismounted. Leading his brown gelding by the reins, he approached the brothers. "Good morning, gentlemen," the officer said. "I am Captain Joshua Tillinghast, and I have come to talk to you about procuring mules for the Army."

Carlos and Juan looked with worried eyes at each other and greeted the officer. "I am Carlos Montoya and this is my brother Juan."

"A pleasure. My commandant gave me your name as a reputable dealer in horses and mules. I believe a local banker recommended you."

"What kind of mule are you looking for, Captain?" Carlos asked, relief in his voice that Juan noticed.

"We are in need of both saddle mules and pack mules for an extended campaign against the Apache."

"How many mules are you looking for?" Carlos asked.

Juan turned and went about the morning chores while Carlos conducted the business of the mules.

"The optimum number is fifty."

"Just plain mules?"

"What do you mean?" the captain asked.

"Do the mules have to be broke to ride and pack?"

"The troopers can break them to ride or pack, whatever is necessary."

"How much are you thinking about paying for these mules?"

"The Army pays market price."

"For me to go out into the country trying to find fifty mules that can be bought for market price could take a year. But, if you want the mules soon, they will cost quite a bit more than market price which is in the neighborhood of ten dollars right now."

"So, you are saying that the mules will cost well over market price?"

"If you want them bought in a couple of months. It will take that long. However, Captain, if you give me an order for fifty mules and will pay twenty-five dollars a head, the word will fly like an eagle and people will bring them in to me, saving a lot of time riding all over the country."

"I doubt if my commandant will pay that much unless the mules are fully trained."

"Perhaps you should talk this over with your commandant and tell me exactly what you want and how much you are willing to pay for these critters."

"I suppose you are correct, Mister Montoya. I will ride back to the fort and see what I can find out."

"Another thing you might discuss with your commandant is the deposit."

"I am not sure whether I know to what you are referring."

"I will need a deposit of five dollars a head with the order before I can go out looking for these mules."

"That seems rather out of the ordinary," the captain said.

"It might seem that way to you but let me explain. If you give me an order for fifty head of mules and I ride out of here looking for them and buy them, I must know you will pay for them when I get them back here. If I do not have a deposit, you might decide to buy the mules from some other dealer and then I am stuck with fifty mules to feed and try to sell at over market price."

"If we give you the order we are not going to buy the mules elsewhere, Mister Montoya."

"It has happened before. I must insist on a deposit or you will need to find some other dealer who needs the business more than I do."

"Should my commandant agree to give you a deposit, how much will it be?"

"Five dollars a head, Captain. If you want fifty head, that will come to two hundred fifty dollars."

"Very well, I will have to ride back to Fort Bleser to see what my commandant says to all this."

"Thank you for stopping by, Captain."

As Carlos went about what was left of the chores with Juan, he explained what had transpired to his brother. He added that he knew about a ranch across the border in Sonora that raised mules for the mines where there was a constant demand for the animals to pull the arrastres used to crush the ore and separate it using mercury. Since the mercury went into the hooves of the mules and made them soon useless, there was quite a turnover.

"If I offer Luis a bonus price, I will be able to buy all fifty head from him and not have to ride over the entire state of Sonora," Carlos said.

"How far is this ranch?" Juan asked.

"A week's ride. If I can get the mules bought I will have to hire some drovers down there, but that should not cost much."

"You haven't got the deposit yet," Juan reminded his brother.

"I think we will see the captain in the morning and he will have two hundred and fifty dollars with him."

Arriving for an early supper so that he could return to the corrals to spend the night, Carlos found María sitting at the kitchen table reading the newspaper. "Where did you find that?" he asked.

"I walked over to the general store and bought it," María said. "There is an advertisement for a teacher at a school called Cuero Quemado. Why is a school named after a burnt hide?"

"That's what folks call a ranch that is southwest of here. It seems a preacher once was in the habit of stealing an occasional beef, which he butchered. He then burned the hide to eliminate the evidence that the beef was stolen. The preacher lived in one of the houses on the ranch. The house was not even as good as a line-camp."

"There are twelve children from first to sixth grade in the school and they want a teacher as soon as possible."

"The Cuero Quemado is a good day's ride from Rinconada. You will have to live there."

"The advertisement says that a house and beef are furnished."

"How much do they pay a teacher out there?"

"It doesn't say. It only says that they will negotiate the salary."

Carlos grunted and moved around to look over Maria's back at the newspaper. "Why not stay here, marry me, and help us with the horses?"

"Carlos, I need to make my own way. It is just something I must prove to myself. I almost fell into a marriage trap with Señor Preston. Now I need to show that I can take care of myself."

"You do not have to prove anything to me. I know you can take care of yourself. You said that you love me. Why are you thinking of going way out there to teach? You may not get to town more than once a month, if that."

María rose from the chair and put her arms around Carlos. He put his hands on her shoulders and kissed her. "Of course, I love you," she said. "I just need some time."

"Time for what?" he asked.

"Time to make sure that I am thinking the right way. I want to be totally sure of myself."

"Does that mean you will marry me?" he asked.

"Once I am sure it is right, yes," she said.

He took her in his arms again and the passion between them rose quickly as their lips joined. Carlos released her and reached around to unbutton the shirtwaist down her back. María felt what he was attempting, twisted around and ducked away from him, putting the table between her and the eager Carlos Montoya.

"I cannot do that yet, Carlos."

"Am I not different than Señor Preston?"

"Certainly you are different than that Tejano. That is not the point. I must not do what my mother said would lower my opinion of myself. After we are married, Carlos. Please understand."

"Again I am thinking that I remember that this has happened to me before," he said.

After supper he returned to the corrals for the night. Try as he might he could not remember where he had tried to take a woman's clothes off.

The following morning after the chores had been completed Carlos saw the army captain riding down Washington Street toward the corrals. "Well Juan, how much would you like to bet that he has our deposit?"

"I do not bet on the American Army."

Dismounting at the hitch rail, Captain Tillinghast strode toward the barn. He walked with his head bent slightly to one side with his sharp chin jutting forward. "Mister Montoya, I discussed the matter of the deposit with my commandant and he has agreed to furnish the two hundred and fifty dollars."

"That is what I need to start getting the fifty mules bought," Carlos said.

"However," the captain continued. "My commandant has ordered me to leave the deposit with the bank until you return with the mules."

"I suppose this is your commandant's way of saying he does not trust Mexicans."

"I have never discussed that question with him," the captain said. "But, you don't seem to trust us to take delivery on the mules once you buy them."

"You are correct. Your army does not always wait for an order to get filled and contracts with more than one dealer."

"If you will come with me to the bank we can set all this up in writing," the captain said.

"No, Captain. I am not going to the bank with you. If you insist on leaving my deposit with the banker, you take care of that. I will see the banker when I finish taking care of some other business. If I do not like what you have written, I will instruct the banker to return your deposit so you can find another dealer."

"Very well, Mister Montoya. I am sorry that you are making this so difficult."

"I am not making things difficult, your commandant is by insisting on leaving the deposit at the bank. In fact, Captain, this entire matter is annoying me greatly. Why not find another dealer who trusts the army."

"I will explain it this way, Mister Montoya. You have been highly recommended for your knowledge of mules and horses as well as for your reputation for honesty. I would hope that you would accept the demands of my commandant. I do not look forward to reporting the failure of my mission, if you know what I mean."

"Sorry, Captain, I have no idea what you mean. I have never been in an army."

"I will return this afternoon depending on what happens in my conversation with my commandant."

"You may tell your commandant that either I have the deposit in my own pocket, or he can find someone else to buy his mules. I have had too much trouble with people in my 'new country'."

The captain returned to the hitch rail, tightened the cinch on his horse and mounted without looking back toward the barn. Carlos and Juan got back to their work of halter breaking four yearlings.

Juan had left for an early supper because it was his turn to sleep in the barn. Carlos had almost finished the evening chores when he saw two soldiers riding down Washington Street. They reined up at the hitch rail, dismounted and began walking toward the barn. Carlos stood by the barn door waiting.

"Mister Montoya, I would like you to meet my commandant, Colonel Briscoe."

"My pleasure, Colonel. I am Carlos Montoya. What can I do for you?"

"Captain Tillinghast tells me that you can buy mules better than anyone around Rinconada."

"I am not in a position to say yes or no to that," Carlos said.

"Captain Tillinghast informs me that you are insisting on a deposit before you go out and purchase the fifty mules."

"That is correct, Colonel. I insist on a deposit every time someone contracts with me for an order."

"When you deal with me, you are dealing with the United States Cavalry."

"All the more reason for a deposit, Colonel. By the time I go out, buy fifty mules and have them driven here, you may have been transferred elsewhere and the new man in charge might tell me to go somewhere else with the mules."

"Let me assure you that that will not happen, Mister Montoya."

"Colonel, I have said what I have said. You know the terms I must have in order to accomplish the contract. Anything else is not acceptable with me. I have told Captain Tillinghast that he should consider finding a dealer he and you can trust. Your government bought this land from Mexico and then made me an American. But, I am still a Mexican in your eyes. I am a Mexican and an American, too. I lost a ranch to a Tejano because I am still a Mexican. I suppose what I am telling you, Colonel, is that I probably do not trust you any more than you trust me. Get yourself a gringo dealer that you can trust."

"Mister Montoya, I am sorry if I have caused you ill feelings. Allow me to make amends."

The Colonel dug into his pocket, withdrew a roll of bills and counted out two hundred and fifty dollars and handed it to Carlos. From his shirt pocket he took a piece of paper and handed it over also. “Sign this receipt and I will trust you to buy fifty mules that will be serviceable as saddle or pack animals,” the colonel said.

“I have a pen in the barn. Come in,” Carlos said, and stuffed the money into his pocket.

The three entered the barn and Carlos went to the small desk where he took the pen and dipped it into the ink well in the corner of the desktop. He signed his full name and handed the paper to the colonel.

“Thank you, Mister Montoya. When will you be starting to look for the mules?”

“I have a few things to clear up before I leave, but I expect I should leave within three days at the longest.”

“How much will these animals cost the U.S. Cavalry?”

“I am not sure until I actually see them and get down to trading with the owners. I estimate that the mules driven here to Rinconada will cost twenty dollars a head minimum and perhaps a bit more, depending on what I have to pay drovers.”

“When can I expect delivery?”

“No later than a month if I have no trouble finding fifty top quality mules that I can buy.”

“I look forward to seeing them,” the colonel said.

Later that morning Carlos visited the bank and discussed the mule order with Will Barlow. “I ought have enough to buy the mules at fifteen dollars a head,” Carlos said as he sat facing the banker.

"That sounds reasonable to me," the banker said. "I can lend you eight hundred for one hundred and twenty days. That gives you a bit extra in case you need it."

"I plan to start in two days if nothing comes up to interfere," Carlos said.

"You seem to be doing well with your horse and mule trading business," the banker said.

"Things are working out. It takes a while before the people get used to honesty in horse trading."

"I know what you mean. Good luck with your venture."

"Thank you. I hope I can repay the loan in less than a hundred and twenty days."

"It's a pleasure doing business with you, Carlos."

"The same."

Carlos stopped by the house to see María for a few minutes, but she was not there. He wondered where she might have gone in the middle of the morning. Back at the corrals he told Juan about the loan. "I hope I can buy mules for fifteen dollars and sell them to the army for twenty," he said.

"You might be able to buy them for less than fifteen, then we would make even more profit," Juan said.

"It will all depend on how many mules the mines in Mexico have used up."

CHAPTER NINE

Arriving home for supper, Carlos stepped up to María and kissed her. "Where did you go this morning?" he asked.

"I went to see Señor Billings about the teaching position that I told you about. He is staying at the Glover Hotel until tomorrow."

"What did he say?"

María smiled. "He said that I can go out there any time, move into the house on the ranch and start teaching."

"That was quick. I must say that I am sad to hear that news," Carlos said, and sat down to the table.

"I have to say that I am happy to have been hired. I do not know how long I will want to be doing this, but for now it seems to be the only acceptable thing a woman can do around here to earn her living."

"I told you that you can stay here and help at the corrals," Carlos said.

"I thought I explained how I felt about taking care of myself."

Carlos looked up at her and smiled as she put his supper on the table. "You explained it very well. I am just trying to talk you into staying here so I do not have to ride all the way out to Cuero Quemado to see you."

María nudged him on his shoulder. "Just think about all the time you will have to think about me while you are riding."

"When are you thinking about moving out there?"

"I suppose I might as well go out there right away and start."

"I will be riding past there in two days. I will ride with you because I cannot bear to think about what Apache raiders might do to a woman riding alone out in that country."

"Why are you going to ride out there in two days?"

"The Cuero Quemado is on the way to a ranch I must visit in Sonora to try and buy fifty head of mules for the army."

"Well, that will work out nicely. You and I did good business today."

Two days later, Carlos led Maria's zebra dun and his packhorse to the house where he loaded Maria's few articles of clothing into one of the panniers on the packsaddle. He also loaded his bedroll and cooking gear along with provisions for his trip to see Luis Alvarez about buying mules at Rancho Piedrado in Sonora. They left the house on Calle Principal at sunrise. Following El Río del Oro south to the pass through the rugged Sierra Cimarrón they kept a steady pace until watering the horses before climbing west over the pass to the Valle de Zacate Alta. At the top of the pass they reined in and turned to look back. "I have been here only three times because Toluca is in the opposite direction," Carlos said. "But this has to be the best view of Rinconada."

"I agree," María said. "I feel like I am going a long way for this teaching position."

"You are," Carlos replied. "That is the biggest reason they have a difficult time keeping teachers at the school there."

Turning back to the trail, they continued to ride over the pass into the valley known for its tall grasses. Toward the center of the valley Carlos reined southward and they rode parallel to a dry stream that Carlos said would have water in it once the rains began again.

They arrived at the Cuero Quemado headquarters with another two hours of sun left for Carlos to ride south with. Briscoe came out of the ranch house to meet them and welcome María to her new home. He showed her the teacher's house and helped carry in her things from Carlos's packhorse. Then he invited them in for supper. Carlos said he needed to keep riding, but María accepted. Briscoe returned to his house and left Carlos and María in the teacher's house.

"Does Briscoe know you are Mexican?" Carlos asked.

"I have no idea what he knows or thinks. He just seems delighted that I accepted the position."

"I had best be riding on, María. I will miss you every minute."

"I will miss you, too, Carlos. Will you stop here on your way back with the mules?"

"I will if I get them bought. One never knows about trading these days with the drought making everything uncommonly dry. It should make it easier to buy livestock to save the owners from feeding them, but I sometimes think that drought affects the minds of humans more than we realize."

"Maybe you can spend more time on the way back," she said.

"I will be able to tell when the time comes. Now, it is time to say good-bye for a while."

He put his arms around her slender waist and pulled her toward him. Kissing her, he wanted to hold her there for an hour, but he released his hold and smiled at her. "María, my beautiful lady, I love you."

"I love you, too, Carlos. Be careful down there."

Carlos left the teacher's house, tightened the cinches on the horses and mounted the bay to try and cover another five miles or so between him and his destination.

Just before the sun began to sink beyond the horizon of rugged desert mountains, he chose a campsite near the streambed that at this point had a small trickle in it. He unsaddled the horses, and led them to the water, damming the trickle with sand to make a puddle big enough for the horses to drink from. He was glad his canteen still held plenty of water for himself.

Once the horses had their fill, he hobbled them and left them to graze the tall, dry grasses that grew near the stream. Not bothering to make a fire, he satisfied his hunger with dried beef mixed with chile that he called machaca. By sunset he had rolled out his bedroll and felt ready for a good night's sleep. Thoughts of María kept him awake for a few moments, but soon he slept soundly until just before first morning light.

He could barely see the horses grazing fifty yards downstream. He started a fire to make morning coffee and went to the dammed puddle for water, but it had washed through. Again he blocked the stream with sand, filled the coffee pot and went back to the fire to get the water boiling.

The sun had not yet risen by the time he had eaten, saddled the horses, packed his gear and stood ready to mount the bay for another day in the saddle.

The following night he spent within the perimeter of a large group of boulders that had been dumped in a sort of circle by some movement of the earth millions of years before. He welcomed the shelter because a wind had sprung up and the boulders shielded him from the dust that seemed to cloud the entire sky.

He rode steadily for five days during the daylight hours until he arrived at Luis Alvarez's Rancho Piedrado. He thought the ranch well named because the terrain for miles around looked like it had been bombarded with volcanic rocks. Piedrado...rocky. Yes, a good name for it. In spite of the rocks, there was sign that the land there supported a good stand of grasses in ordinary times. But, Carlos could see that most of the grasses had been eaten down to the roots. Drought.

He approached the headquarters, being careful to allow the occupants of the small adobe house to see him from a distance once the dogs began sounding their alarms. He waited for some sign of life before venturing more than a hundred yards further.

A hatless old man opened the worn wooden door hinged to its frame with rawhide and appeared, shielding his eyes from the sun to discover who his visitor might be. His nearly white hair fluttered in the breeze. Carlos booted the bay to get started again. When he came within ten yards of the ocotillo fence that enclosed the house and yard, he reined in again and spoke a greeting. "Hola," he said. "I am Carlos Montoya from Rinconada. I came to look at your mules. Do you have any for sale?"

"Come in," the man said. "Get down from your horse. Yes I have some mules for sale. The mines are not taking them fast enough during this dry time and the feed is getting scarce."

Carlos liked what he heard. Perhaps he could buy mules even cheaper than he had thought if Alvarez was anxious to get them off his range. He dismounted, tied the two horses to the hitch rail and followed Alvarez into the house. Inside he nodded to an old lady who stood in front of a cast iron cook stove making tortillas as she watched a pot of beans simmer. Alvarez offered him a chair at the kitchen table, the only table in the house that could be used for meals. Carlos sat down across from the rancher and the woman brought two old chipped mugs full of inky black coffee. Alvarez pushed a dish with brownish sugar over to Carlos who spooned in a good measure with the wooden spoon and stirred it. He pushed the dish to Alvarez who put twice as much sugar in his mug.

"Have the rains come to your country?" Alvarez asked.

"No, it is as dry as flour. I see this part of Sonora has not seen rain in quite a while."

"It has not rained on this ranch in eight months. I have one waterhole left because the others all dried up into dust."

"It will rain some day, it always does," Carlos said.

"It better rain soon or I will not be around here to see it. How many mules are you looking for to buy?" Alvarez asked.

"If you have the right kind I can buy fifty head. That is if the price is right."

"I have at least fifty top quality mules. We can ride out to the waterhole in the morning. They will all be there. We will have supper soon and I have a friendly bottle of mescal to talk over."

"That will taste good after the ride I have made to get here," Carlos said.

"You can put up your horses in the corrals over by the barn. I am sorry that we do not have an extra room in this house, but you are welcome to unroll your bed here in the kitchen."

"That will be fine," Carlos said, glancing at the packed dirt floor.

After they finished the coffee, Carlos left the house and led the horses to the corrals, unsaddled them and took some grain from one of the panniers to put in the feed trough. A mule in the adjoining corral walked over to see who the company was. Carlos looked him over and hoped that the fifty in the pasture were as good as this one that Alvarez used for himself.

Returning to the house, Carlos found Alvarez sitting at the table as before only now with a plate full of food in front of him. There was a plate where Carlos had been sitting before taking care of his horses. "Sit down and have some supper," Alvarez said.

"Gracias, Carlos replied. "It is nice to have a good meal after traveling for five days."

"This is venison birria," Alvarez said. "I shot a doe three days ago by the water hole that we will go to in the morning. There was very little fat on her with the feed so scarce."

"What condition are your mules in?" Carlos asked.

"They are not fat," Alvarez said, and continued eating the meal as he rolled the pieces of spicy meat into a corn tortilla.

The last of Rancho Piedrado's precious water holes caught spring water at the base of a small range of mountains. From the ranch headquarters it took two hours to cover the distance.

"Most of them are still out grazing," Alvarez said. "We can either wait here for them to come in for water or go out and look for them."

"I say wait here and look at them as they arrive," Carlos said. "Those over there under that mesquite tree look like the kind of mules I am looking for."

"Those eight are good mules. And do you notice those two jacks with those mares?"

"Yes, they are good sized jackasses," Carlos said.

"That is what it takes to get good size on a mule, but the mare is just as important. If the mare is short legged the mule foal will probably be short legged even with a long legged jack. Sometimes it makes no sense at all how the foal turns out."

"It is the same for horses," Carlos said.

"Look toward that canyon. Here comes a lot of them down from the mountains," Alvarez said. "There must be thirty head."

Carlos watched the mules mixed with mares and a few mule foals as they plodded toward the waterhole. He saw that their condition reflected the drought. However, the army had plenty of hay and grain to feed them and their bones structure looked good.

As soon as that bunch arrived and drank their fill of water, another group arrived from a different direction north of the canyon. There were no mares in this bunch, just mules. There were forty-four. Five of them were younger than the others, but they had good conformation. *Now, if I can get these mules bought right, we can make some money on this deal.*

"Why are the mines not buying mules?" Carlos asked as they looked at the last bunch to wander in.

"They have had problems keeping miners. A lot of them have gone to the United States mines where the pay is better."

"Have the Mexican mines shut down?"

"No, just slowed down. I think also that they are running short of silver ore and have to mine other things. They are probably using mules for pack animals rather than working in the arrastres where the mercury eats away at the mules' hooves."

Carlos could see that the market for mules in Mexico had dropped off regardless of the drought. The drought made it even tougher on the rancher trying to keep animals when they should be sold to conserve feed and water.

"How much are you asking for your mules, my choice?"

"Your choice? I think twelve dollars, oro."

"All I have is American money. We don't use plata much anymore. Twelve dollars seems far too high since I will buy fifty mules that you will not have to worry about drinking up the rest of your water here."

"I am used to getting ten dollars straight run from the mines."

"But the mines have quit buying," Carlos countered. "I am thinking that seven dollars is tops and I must have the choice. I never buy mules on a straight run basis. A bad one always seems to run into the line as it goes for the count."

"Seven dollars is too low," Alvarez complained.

"I can tell you, Señor, when my buyer sees how poor these mules are, I will be lucky to get paid for the trip."

"When will you take delivery?"

"If you and I can drive these mules to your corrals today and I can cut out the fifty I want, I will pay you five dollars to help me drive them to Rinconada starting tomorrow."

"How about nine dollars?"

"Seven dollars is my top dollar. It is either seven or I ride on to the next ranch that raises mules."

"The Hernandez mules are not as good as mine," Alvarez said.

Carlos had never heard of the Hernandez ranch. "But, I will bet you I can buy fifty for seven dollars a head or less."

Carlos reined his bay away from the waterhole. "Sorry we cannot make a deal, Señor."

"Wait a moment," Alvarez said. "Will you pay in cash?"

"Of course," Carlos replied. He knew then that he had bought the mules for seven dollars a head.

"All right. There is one more small bunch missing. They should be here soon."

The two men sat on their respective mounts and waited for ten more minutes. As Alvarez predicted, the last of the mule herd arrived with several mares and a jack. Carlos noticed that there were less foals than he thought there would be. Drought.

They circled around the animals, some lying down in the shade of the surrounding mesquite trees, and yelled at them to get moving. Carlos had the thought that it is always easier to drive cattle and horses to water than away from water. Mules could not be any different in that aspect. As much as possible they cut back the mares, foals, yearlings and jacks. By the time they had lined them out on the trail back to the ranch headquarters they had only a few mares in the bunch. Carlos slipped the bay in behind three mares without foals and cut them out of the herd. Not wanting to spook any of the mules that he wanted to buy, he reined the bay back to the rear of the column.

The mules soon resigned themselves to being driven and plodded along, many with their long ears flopping back and forth and their tails swatting flies. Arriving at the corrals, Alvarez loped ahead and opened the gate leading to the main corral. Then he reined his mule down from the gate to direct the herd into the corral. Carlos continued to push them along until all were inside and the gate closed and latched.

"We should cut out those three mares with their foals and the five yearlings," Alvarez said. "Then you can go in and cut out the mules you do not want. Did you get a count as we drove them home here?"

"I counted seventy-two mules, but I might be off one or two since they were strung out pretty far."

"I counted seventy-two, so if we cut out twelve and then make another count on the fifty you are buying we should be all right. Then we can turn the twelve out to go back to the mountains. They will hurry because I will not give them any water here. I have a shallow dug well that furnishes us a bare minimum during these dry times."

"Will there be enough for the fifty and our saddle stock?"

"I think so. It takes a while to haul the bucket to the top and put the water in the trough."

Carlos held the gate into a second corral where they put the mares, foals and yearlings. Alvarez opened the gate from that corral to the pasture and released those animals. They all headed back to the mountains.

Carlos rode in among the mules, looking them over closely to determine which he wanted and which he did not want. After scrutinizing the herd for fifteen minutes, he began cutting those that were to remain at Rancho Piedrado. The first mule he cut back had a slight limp. The second had watery eyes that had yellow puss in the corners and kept shaking its head every so often. The rest he cut back on the basis of height and general conformation. Up close they did not look as thin as they did around the waterhole.

When Carlos finished choosing the mules he wanted to buy, he and Alvarez counted them carefully. Both had fifty. Alvarez asked if Carlos was satisfied with the cut and Carlos waved. The rancher opened the gate again and let the cutbacks loose into the pasture. The two men walked to the house and enjoyed coffee as they settled up their business.

We should fill the water trough so they get water through the night," Alvarez said. "I have a little hay in the barn. I saved it for emergencies. I will feed some to the mules because they will not get much to eat on the trip to Rinconada."

Carlos said nothing about the area just north of what looked like the border that had a mesa with a good stand of grass. He figured to drive the mules to the mesa and let them graze overnight even if it meant little sleep for him and Alvarez.

At the well, they took turns winching up the bucket full of water and pouring it into a wooden sluiceway that went to the water trough. They spent an hour at that chore. "These mules have either developed a thirst during the drive down from the mountains or they want to see us work," Carlos said.

Alvarez did not see the humor in what Carlos said. "It will be their last night on Rancho Piedrado. I do not want to see them leave thirsty."

Carlos could see that the rancher held affection for his animals. Then he wondered why Alvarez ever sold the mules to the mines where they were not treated well working every day on the Arrastres.

Before going to the house, Alvarez went into the barn and brought enough hay to fill the bunks built against the barn wall that formed one side of the corral. Carlos thought that the hay was probably more than the mules had eaten in weeks.

The following morning they began the drive to Rinconada by opening the corral gate and starting the mules in the opposite direction from the mountains where they had been. At first there were several that wanted to go their own way back to familiar country, but with Carlos and Alvarez there to discourage them, the mules strung out heading north. Alvarez knew that one of the mules was a born leader, so had buckled a bell around its neck. The rest followed well.

They spent the first two nights with ranchers who Alvarez knew. Carlos was glad that they could pen the mules in corrals and save taking turns watching them at night so they would not wander too far away in their search for feed.

When they arrived below the mesa that had the ample stand of grass, Carlos showed it to Alvarez and they agreed it would make a perfect place to let the mules graze overnight. The men took turns riding around the herd as the animals filled their bellies on the dried grasses.

The next stretch of the trip had no water for their animals, but they kept them moving until they reached the Cuero Quemado, where water remained plentiful from a reliable well that went down eighty feet to a small aquifer.

Carlos went to Maria's small house as soon as they had settled the mules in the corral. Billings had come out to meet them and told them that they were welcome to spend the night, and to be sure and come to the headquarters for supper. "I will invite María to join us," Billings said.

María stood outside the door to the house waiting for Carlos to walk in from the corrals. When he came close, she ran out to meet him with her arms spread out like she wanted to fly. They embraced one another and kissed.

"I have missed you every minute since you rode out of here," María said.

"I have missed you, too."

"I see you bought your mules," she said.

"Yes. I bought them right, but do not say anything to the man I rode in with because I bought the mules from him. I am paying him to help drive them into Rinconada."

"Carlos, I am so happy to see you."

"I think about you most of the time when I am riding to and from somewhere," Carlos said. "When we have finished supper, I would like to take a walk with you away from the house so we can be alone."

"I would like that, too," She said. "But we must be careful not to arouse any suspicions from Mister Billings because I think he is probably more strict than I am."

"It will not be for very long because I need some sleep for tomorrow's ride into Rinconada."

CHAPTER TEN

Carlos and Alvarez arrived at the Montoya corrals just before sunset. Juan opened the gate to the largest corral and stood back so as not to spook the mules into scattering. The mules plodded on at their usual pace in spite of the distance they had walked in five days. Smelling the water in the long trough on one side of the corral they hastened to stick their noses into its coolness and quench their thirst.

"Hola," Juan said as Carlos rode up to the corral.

"Hola. It is good to be back. Juan this is Luis Alvarez from whom I bought the mules."

Luis nodded and spoke his name.

"I am glad to see you found some mules. Your friend was here today wondering when you would be back. I think he is staying at the Glover tonight."

"Good," Carlos said. "I will go there tonight and tell him he can come by in the morning. These mules can use some hay and grain."

"I can see that," Juan said. "They look like good animals in spite of their condition."

"The country down there is drier than it is here. I will give the bay some water and then ride to the Glover to find our friend. Take Luis to the house and feed him. He can sleep in Maria's room. Get him going early in the morning so he does not meet our friend at the corrals."

"Have our friend show up around noon if you can, just to make sure."

Carlos rode the bay over to the water trough. There were still mules lined up but the bay nudged his way in between them and took a long drink. When he lifted his head from the trough, Carlos reined him back and left the corral for the Glover Hotel.

He found the colonel in the bar sitting at a small table with the captain. The colonel looked up as Carlos approached the table and greeted him. "I was talking to your brother this morning asking when he thought you would return with the mules," the colonel said.

"We got in about a half an hour ago with fifty mules. Come over tomorrow morning and you can pick them up."

"That will be fine," the colonel said.

"I will see you tomorrow," Carlos said.

"Can I buy you a drink?" the colonel asked. "After a trail drive like you've been on I should think a good drink would be in order."

"I think you are right," Carlos said. "A nice shot of mescal should chase the dust out of my throat."

"Sit down," the colonel said, and motioned to the waiter who hurried to the table.

"Yes, Colonel?"

"Bring my friend a double shot of mescal, if you will."

"Yes sir."

Carlos sat down between the colonel and the captain, nodding to Tillinghast.

"Did you run into any trouble on the trail?" the colonel asked.

"None. It is a long way to get there, but I found your mules. The drought is bad down there, but the mules are sound and should work out for you once they flesh up some."

"I hear the drought is the most severe in years," Tillinghast said.

"Sometimes I wonder if we are always in a drought and that every once in a while it rains," Carlos said.

The colonel laughed at Carlos's humor. The waiter brought the glass of mescal and put it on the table in front of Carlos. He took the glass in his right hand and held it up toward the two army officers. "Salud!" he said, and brought the glass to his lips. He took a good-sized swallow and put the glass back on the table.

"I have been asking around about you, Carlos. As you have told me, I understand your family once owned a sizeable ranch that was a Spanish land grant."

"Yes, it was our home for several generations until the Texan Preston somehow grabbed it away from us."

"There was some question about the deed, I believe," the colonel said.

"The records burned many years ago in Arispe. Colonel, if you do not mind I would just as soon talk about something else."

Carlos lifted the glass up to his lips again and finished the contents. "In fact, I should get back and put my horse up. He has been on the trail for ten days. Goodnight, Colonel, Captain. I will plan to see you tomorrow. Thank you for the drink."

Carlos rose from his chair, left the bar in the Glover Hotel and rode back to the corrals. Juan met him and told him that Alvarez had gone to the house and devoured a large bowl of beans. Carlos unsaddled the bay and put him in a stall with a generous measure of grain and hay. "Tomorrow, my friend, you will not have to go anywhere," he said to the horse.

Alvarez joined them for an early breakfast, saddled up and left the corrals before sunrise. Carlos and Juan wondered why the old man had not done any shopping in Rinconada while he had the chance. "I think he may be thinking that spending money when the market for his mules is so bad is not the wise thing to do," Carlos said.

"But, he is a long ride from anywhere, is he not?"

"Yes. And, you should see how frugally he and his wife live. I will bet he still has that five dollars I paid him six months from now."

"He will probably have half that carne seca you gave him for the trail by the time he gets home," Juan said.

"That is the way those old timers are. They have gone through tough times and they remember," Carlos said. "I am glad I did not feel sorry for him living way out there on that rock pile."

"Why is that?" Juan asked.

"I might have paid him ten dollars a head for the mules instead of seven."

The mules savored the hay that Juan and Carlos had tossed into the feed bunks. Their bellies had filled enough to make the gaunt condition of yesterday diminish, but they remained thin.

Colonel Briscoe and Captain Tillinghast rode in an hour after sunrise. As they watched the two officers approach, Carlos said, "I am glad we said good bye to Alvarez before they got here."

"I had the same thought, Juan said.

The officers dismounted at the hitch rail and secured their horses before approaching Carlos and Juan at the barn.

"Good morning, gentlemen," Briscoe said.

"Good morning to you," Carlos replied. "Come with us into the large corral and see what I brought you."

Carlos opened the gate and motioned the two officers to go through into the enclosure where the mules crowded along the feed bunk munching on the remaining hay the Montoyas had forked in for their breakfast.

The two officers stood looking at the mules. Carlos walked over and made the animals move out into the corral where the officers could get a better look at them. Juan stood by the feed bunk to keep the mules away.

"I must say, Montoya, these mules are a sorry lot," Briscoe said. "They look like they haven't had a blade of grass for six months."

"Well, Colonel Briscoe, if you had seen the country they came from you would probably have concluded that these mules had eaten all the little rocks and started on the big ones."

"Why did you bring them to sell to me?"

"They are the best around. The drought has been tough, especially down where I found these animals. If you will look at them carefully, you will see that they are well framed and strong legged. You will not find better mules anywhere these days."

"It will take a month of Sundays to get their flesh back," Briscoe said with disdain.

"Considering they came off a dry rock pile of a ranch without any sort of supplement, I would say they are exceptional animals," Carlos said.

"And you told me these critters will cost the Army twenty dollars a head?"

"That is correct, Colonel. That is our deal. But you got something extra."

"Good heavens, what could that be, the gold in their tails?"

Carlos did not smile or even hesitate to continue. "Every one of these mules is broke to lead. That will save you lots of time since they are fully-grown. If they had not been halter broke your troopers would have one big rodeo. I should probably charge you five dollars a head for the training they have received."

"I am not sure if I will take delivery on these mules," Briscoe said. "If the general comes by before we get them fleshed up, he will give me a complete dressing down before God and everybody."

"As far as I am concerned, Colonel, these are your mules. I did the very best I could to get the best quality mules there are around the country. I rode five days to find them and five days driving them here."

"I suppose you are right, Montoya. But, it is going to take a lot of groceries to get these starved out critters ready for service."

"You can use that time to break them to ride or pack, whatever you decide on," Carlos said. "I would like to get paid for these mules now so you can drive them out to Fort Bleser."

"I will give you a letter of procurement that you can send to general headquarters. They, in turn, will send you a voucher that you can deposit."

"Now, wait just a minute, Colonel. I want the money before you drive these mules out of my corrals. After today I will have to charge you twenty-five cents a day feed bill and a dollar a day rent on the corral space."

"That is preposterous, Montoya."

"You may think so, Colonel, but I have a business to run here. Just because you are used to army methods does not mean I am. I am barely getting used to American methods. Cash, Colonel, or a whopping feed bill in addition to the twenty dollars a head for the mules."

"I cannot possibly give you cash," Briscoe said. "The best I can do is provide you with a voucher that you can deposit with Mister Barlow if he so chooses to cash it."

"If that is the case, Colonel, we might as well go to the bank right now and see what Mister Barlow has to say because these mules are not leaving this corral unless I have the money for them."

"Very well, Captain Tillinghast and I will meet you at the bank in half an hour."

The officers walked toward the gate. Juan opened it and let them out into the alleyway between corrals. Carlos went to the stall where the bay relaxed with his hay. "Sorry, my friend, I told you that today you were not going anywhere. It is just a short trip to the bank."

He saddled the bay and mounted. Juan stood by the barn door. "Do you need me with you?"

"I do not think so. These cabrones seem to think Mexicans are stupid. No money, no mules. I think they believe me at last."

"They do not know that the banker lent you money to buy the mules and wants his loan paid back," Juan said.

"That is what I am counting on. Too bad these army people do not have to make a living trading horses and mules. Their attitudes might be different."

"Well, Brother, good luck," Juan said.

Carlos reined away to Washington Street. He wanted to reach the bank before the army did. The hitch rail in front of The Territorial Bank stood vacant when he rode up. Dismounting, he wrapped the reins around the rail, stepped up onto the boardwalk and opened the door to the bank. Will Barlow looked up from his desk as Carlos entered. The banker rose from his chair and went to meet his customer. "You're back sooner than I thought you would be," Barlow said. "How did your trip go?"

“Everything went quite well, Mister Barlow. I bought fifty mules and drove them back. The colonel and his captain will be here shortly. He says he wants to give me some sort of voucher to pay for the mules. Sir, I do not know what he is talking about. First he wanted to give me some letter to send to his headquarters and then they would send me a voucher. I told him he must pay me cash. I need to pay back the money you lent me and I cannot do that with some piece of paper.”

“I can give you cash for a government voucher, Carlos,” Barlow said. “When you do business with the U.S. government you need to charge plenty for the trouble they put you through to get your money. Eventually the money will arrive, but it is difficult to carry on a business and have to wait for people to pay their bills, and that includes the government.”

“I also told the colonel that I would charge him twenty-five cents a day feed bill and a dollar a day for the corral if he does not get those mules out of there before tomorrow.”

“Smart move,” Barlow said. “Sometimes military people forget that civilians cannot count on a paymaster coming around.”

The conversation stopped as the door opened and the officers entered the bank. Barlow greeted them and invited them to sit down in his fenced in office area. After everyone had seated themselves, Barlow opened the meeting. “I understand you are here to give Mister Montoya a government voucher for the mules he sold to you.”

“I have it right here,” Colonel Briscoe said, taking an envelope out of his pocket. “I believe that is the correct amount.”

Briscoe handed the voucher to Carlos who saw the amount of seven hundred fifty dollars written after his name. Carlos handed the voucher to Barlow. “Is that the correct amount, Carlos?”

“Yes, Mister Barlow.”

“I will deposit this to your account then if you will sign your name on the bottom line. There,” he said as he pointed to the line at the bottom of the voucher.

Carlos took the voucher and the pen, dipped the pen in the ornate ink well on the banker’s desk and signed his name.

“Thank you, Mister Barlow, and thank you, Colonel. When will you be at the corrals to get your mules?”

“I will have to get some troopers to help.”

“I have an idea,” Carlos said. “My brother, Juan, and I will help you drive the mules to Fort Bleser and there will be no extra charge.”

“That sounds fine. When do you want to start?”

“That depends on you. We can start anytime,” Carlos said. “I need to talk with Mister Barlow a minute and then I will ride back to the corrals and tell Juan what we will be doing.”

“We will meet you at the corral in an hour,” Briscoe said. “We have to check out of the hotel.”

The officers rose and left the bank. Carlos remained with Barlow. “I can pay you back for the loan, Mister Barlow.”

"You don't have to. I loaned it for one hundred and twenty days and you have only been gone for ten days. There is no hurry."

"I would just as soon pay off the loan."

"Fine. I will take it out of this deposit. You certainly did well on this transaction."

"I think it turned out all right. There were ten days of hard riding in there to earn it."

"If you paid fifteen dollars a head for the mules and sold them for twenty, you made a nice profit," Barlow said.

"I did better than that," Carlos said, but did not tell the banker how much he had paid Alvarez for his mules.

"Incidentally, Carlos, I don't know if you have heard that Hungerford is trying to sell his livery stable along with his horses and buggies," Barlow said. "Would you be interested?"

"I heard some rumors that he wanted to sell," Carlos said. "I cannot say that I am interested in expanding. The reason he wants to sell is that the horses he maintains are a pretty sorry lot. A month ago one of his buggies broke an axle five miles from town and forced the passengers to walk in."

"I understand," Barlow said. "Sometimes it is best to keep going at the same pace. You are probably wise to let the cards fall where they will."

"My grandfather once cautioned me against greed. He lived a lot of life," Carlos said.

"I wish I had known him, but he died before I arrived in Rinconada. Many people still speak well of Ysidoro

Montoya even though he has been gone for a number of years."

"I had better get back to the corrals and tell Juan about the work I arranged for him and me."

"I hope the drive to the fort is uneventful."

"I do, too. I do not care to tangle with Apache raiders who love to eat mule steaks."

Carlos left the bank and rode back to the corral. He told Juan about his offer to help the army officers drive the mules to Fort Bleser, so Juan saddled a gray gelding that he had been training for a month.

"You take the point when we get them going," Carlos said. "I will ride flank so I can chase them away from the petunias in front of the houses. Take them up the river until you get to Tamarindo Creek, then head them east to the fort."

"What are you going to do, put those officers in the rear drag and watch them eat mule dust?" Juan asked, and smiled.

"We are doing this for no pay so we should not have to eat dust as well," Carlos said.

The colonel and the captain rode down Washington Street to the corrals. Carlos told them his plan for the drive and opened the gate to let the mules out. Juan rode out a ways to be in place when the animals began to leave through the opened gate. Carlos rode into the corral and started the mules toward the gate. The officers waited outside to take up the rear. When all the mules had vacated the corral, Carlos rode up and shut the gate.

Two mules near the rear tried to cut back. Perhaps they thought they were being driven too far away from the feed bunk. Carlos chased them back into the bunch. The hooves churned up the powdery dust from the flood plain of the river. There was no wind to whisk it away so the officers became engulfed in the cloud. Carlos looked around and could barely see them through the dust. As the column neared the yards of several houses still within the town limits, Carlos kept the mules away from the gardens of flowers and vegetables that had not been fenced.

Reaching Tamarindo Creek in two hours, Juan turned east and the lead mule followed him as if he had been ordered to. Tamarindo Creek debauched into the Rinconada River in a broad fan like delta. There was no stream flow when the column of mules entered its dry sandy bed. Thick groves of mesquite lined the Creek for a mile up stream. Carlos had ridden it many times looking for stray cattle after the gathers at Toluca.

Suddenly, the third mule from the point stumbled and fell, followed by the distinct sound of a rifle shot. Juan and Carlos looked quickly in the direction of the sound. “Apache,” Carlos yelled to Juan and then again to the officers in the rear.

Carlos pulled his carbine quickly from its scabbard, crouched low over the neck of the bay and booted him into a run toward the sound, but the mesquite bosque, too thick to penetrate, blocked his advance. Dismounting, he led the bay through spaces in between the trees. After twenty yards of being scratched by the thorny branches he spotted a single warrior bent low to avoid the tree branches, trying to leave the scene as quickly as possible.

Carlos stopped, shouldered the carbine, took aim and fired. He saw the Indian spin and almost fall and then another Indian came out of the trees and grabbed his companion by one arm to get him out of the way and behind the trunk of a large mesquite. Carlos ejected the casing and levered a new one into the chamber. Before he could squeeze off another shot he felt his shoulder burn. He glanced at the pain and saw an arrow sticking in from behind. He dropped to the ground and looked around to try and discover where the other Apache might be.

Juan came quickly to his side, dropping down beside his brother. “What the devil happened?” Juan asked.

“I got one and then one of his friends came and grabbed him. As I was trying to get off another shot, this arrow hit my shoulder from behind.”

“Where are they?” Juan asked.

“I am not sure now, but I think they are trying to get away from us. They probably figure we will leave the dead mule so they will be back to bone the poor devil out once we are gone with the rest. Apache cabrones!”

“The arrow came through and did not hit bone,” Juan said. “I think I can pull it clear through if you can stand the pain.”

“That pain would be much better than having to ride to Fort Bleser with the arrow in my shoulder. Look around and see if those cabrones have high tailed it to the hills.”

Juan walked in a crouched position, looking in all directions as he went. Behind the big mesquite where his friend had shoved the wounded Indian, Juan saw a large amount of blood on the ground. He returned to Carlos. “There is plenty of blood on the ground behind that big mesquite. You got him, all right. I hope you killed him.”

“Did you see any signs of them?” Carlos asked.

“Nothing. I think they must have gotten to their horses and left for the hills.”

“All right, Brother, see if you can pull this arrow through without taking the rest of my shoulder with it.”

“Cut the feathers off first,” Carlos said.

Juan positioned Carlos against a long growing mesquite limb so that the arrow’s shaft lay against it. He took his knife and a rock from the ground. Placing the sharp edge of the knife on the wooden shaft he pounded the knife’s dull edge with the rock. The second blow severed the arrow’s shaft.

Carlos groaned, then gritted his teeth and clamped down with his jaws, anticipating the pain of the arrow getting pulled through the flesh of his shoulder. Juan put his left hand on his brother’s shoulder so that the shaft of the arrow was between his thumb and forefinger. Then he grabbed the shaft just behind the arrowhead and pulled the arrow through the wound as quickly as he could without tearing any more flesh than he had to.

“Aye, chingado!” Carlos cried out. “It felt like a hot iron.”

"Hold on a minute," Juan said. "I am going to rip my shirt sleeve off for a bandage to stop the bleeding."

Juan took off his shirt and with his knife, cut the left sleeve off and fashioned a bandage for his brother's shoulder. When he had it bound up as best he could he helped Carlos away from the bosque with the bay following. "Do you think you can ride?" Juan asked.

"I am certainly not going to walk," Carlos replied. "We had better find the mules."

"Here, Juan said, handing Carlos the two pieces of the arrow. "Keep this as a memento."

Juan looked upstream once he had mounted the gray. "The officers are still driving them, but they are at least a quarter mile ahead."

"It was nice of them to wait for us to be killed," Carlos said.

When the Montoya brothers caught up to the column of mules they found the officers pushing their charges as fast as they could without the mules breaking into a run. Carlos and Juan rode up to them. "Are the mules all here?" Carlos asked.

"All but the one the bastards killed," Briscoe said. "What the hell happened to your shoulder?"

"I caught an arrow. Juan pulled it through. Here are the pieces," he said, showing them to the colonel.

"Where in hell are the Apaches?"

"They are probably up in the hills waiting for us to get far enough away so they can come down and bone out their groceries," Carlos said.

"I must say, Montoya," Briscoe said. "You showed a heap of courage going into that mesquite thicket after those bastards."

"I got one. I do not know how badly, but there was blood behind a mesquite where he hid for a moment. I hope I killed him."

"You sound like you don't like Apaches," the colonel said.

"They killed our mother and father along with our sister," Carlos said. "Why should I like them? I will kill every one of them that I possibly can."

"I am glad they only managed to kill one of the mules," Briscoe said.

"They are just shopping," Carlos said.

"We would have been with you, but I thought it best to guard the mules from those bastards," Briscoe said.

"You did the right thing, Colonel. Have you ever killed an Apache?"

"Not yet, but I hope to get out in the field very soon."

"You will be lucky to even see one of them, much less get a shot at one. They can hide so well that you can pass within feet of a hiding Apache and never see him."

"I have heard about their wily ways," Briscoe said. "This might be a good opportunity to go after them for killing our mule."

"By the time you can get a troop ready to go after them, they will be far away in country you never imagined existed," Carlos said.

"They couldn't be that difficult to find if we have competent trackers."

Carlos almost laughed at the colonel's point of view of the Apache raiders. "Colonel, you do what you want to do. Remember that having lived here for many generations they know every inch of this country."

Carlos reined the bay around the mules to take the point at the head of the column. Juan had changed to ride the flank position. They reached Fort Bleser in less than two hours. The troopers stopped whatever they were doing to watch the mules arrive. Carlos saw them talking to each other and knew they were commenting on the animals they would soon be working with.

Colonel Briscoe took Carlos to the surgeon and had his shoulder properly bandaged and dressed. The doctor insisted that Carlos wear a sling to keep the arm from moving and breaking the clots at each end of the wound.

After the session with the doctor, Carlos and Juan enjoyed a noon meal with the officers. By early afternoon they began heading back to Rinconada. Once away from the fort and riding along Tamarindo Creek, Carlos suggested that they keep on the south side rather than risk happening on the Indians dressing out the mule carcass. They found a trail that weaved its way through the south *bosque* and kept them hidden from anyone riding along the north side of the creek. When they reached the point opposite where the mule had met its end, they dismounted, took their carbines from their scabbards and crept through the trees toward the creek. There across the creek six Apaches worked quickly cutting the meat from the bones of the mule and loading it onto two horses.

“I told you this is what they would do,” Carlos whispered.

“We could probably kill two of them,” Juan whispered back.

“We might kill two and then we might have to make a stand against the other four. Best we get back to our horses and go home.”

Once again mounted, they remained silent for a mile, not wanting to alarm the Indians. Finally Carlos broke the silence. “There must have been at least seven to begin with because I did not see the one I wounded helping with the meat.”

“Maybe that one is dead,” Juan said.

“We will never know because I am not curious enough to try to find out,’ Carlos said, and laughed. “I keep feeling vengeful against them for killing our parents and sister, but I also seem to remember Grandfather and someone else cautioning me against revenge.”

“How do you mean?” Juan asked.

“That revenge never solved anything, that it only created more trouble and problems.”

“Sounds reasonable,” Juan said.

After reaching Rinconada and the corrals, the brothers fed the horses, fixed their supper, and Juan returned to the barn to make sure the Apache shoppers did not try to steal anything more. He hooked up the alarm bell to the gates with the wire and went to bed for the night, his carbine standing up by the door to the room.

CHAPTER ELEVEN

A month after Carlos and Juan helped deliver the army mules, María came to town with the Billings family in their buckboard. Carlos watched Mister and Missus Billings sitting on the seat, with María and the three children in the back. Billings reined in the team by the corrals as Carlos hastened out from the barn to meet María.

She jumped down from the buckboard, took her valise by its handle, and lowered it to the ground. "I am sorry that things did not work out, Mister Billings," María was saying as Carlos arrived. "I hope you can find someone else to teach out there."

"It is too bad you can't stay," Missus Billings said. "The children liked you very much."

Billings sat on the seat of the buckboard looking straight ahead without saying a word. He slapped the reins on the rumps of the team and the buckboard continued on its way up Washington Street.

María turned to Carlos with her arms outstretched. He took her into his arms and kissed her. "I missed you terribly," María said. "But that is not the only reason I decided to come back to Rinconada."

"You have me all curious," Carlos said. "Can we go up to the barn and talk?"

"Oh yes, I am just all happy to be back here with you."

Carlos reached down, picked up her valise and carried it as they walked up to the barn and into the room where María had stayed after leaving Toluca. They sat on the cot.

"Now I know why Mister Billings has a difficult time keeping teachers out there so far from town," María said. "He cannot keep his hands to himself."

"What do you mean?" Carlos asked.

"It did not start until two weeks ago. He came over to my little house without an invitation. After knocking on the door he just walked in. The first thing I thought was what if I had been standing naked in the middle of the room?"

"Were you dressed?"

"Yes, thank goodness. He started telling me how he thought I was the most beautiful woman he had ever seen. I asked him to leave, but he continued talking to me as if he had not heard what I had said. Then he came toward me and grabbed my shoulders."

"I think I know what happened next," Carlos said.

"The same thing that I did to Mister Preston when he tried to have me. Mister Billings roared like a wounded bull just as Mister Preston did. I ran out the door and hid behind that big tree you saw off to the left of the schoolhouse. He left my house holding his privates and went to the barn."

"Why the barn?"

"I suppose he did not want Missus Billings to see him in agony."

"When did all this happen?"

"Yesterday. I told him this morning that I wanted to leave immediately. He told me I would have to wait a week until he was ready to make a trip into town. I told him that if he did not take me with his family into town today, I would tell everything to Missus Billings. That seemed to be the best I could do."

"It worked," Carlos said. "And I am very happy to see you, María."

"What is that bulge on your shoulder?"

"It is a bandage. When Juan and I helped deliver the mules to Fort Bleser I caught an Apache arrow. It is just about healed."

"Good heavens, you could have been killed." she said.

"A lot of people have been, but I am lucky," he said, trying to lessen her anxiety.

"Well, I guess you now have a hired hand here at the corrals," she said, and smiled. "That is what you wanted, was it not?"

Carlos smiled, leaned over and kissed her cheek and took her hand in his. "I am anxious to see how you can train some colts I bought before I went to Rancho Piedrado for the mules. There are three of them and they should make good saddle stock."

"I look forward to that in the morning," she said. "I think I would like to go to the house now. By the way, how much do you pay woman trainers?"

"I have not thought about that," Carlos said. "Why not marry me so we do not have to get involved with money?"

"Carlos Montoya, you are a devil."

They went to the house on Calle Principal where Juan had cooked a supper of *birria* made from goat meat. He welcomed María and seemed surprised that she had decided to leave the Cuero Quemado School. Carlos told him she had very good reasons and that seemed to satisfy him.

After supper, Juan went to the barn to sleep. Carlos and María decided to have a stroll through town to see what might be going on in the early evening. They returned after dark and María fixed a pot of coffee. Carlos sat by the table in the kitchen.

"You have not given me an answer, María," he said.

"I know that. I am still thinking about it."

"Hmm."

María sat down in a chair across from him. "I suppose I need to clear up some thinking on my part," María said. "I have this real need to prove to myself that I can take care of myself. By that I mean to make a living as well as to survive in a world full of violence and vengefulness. I took that teaching position as part of that desire and need. It did not work out, just as getting married to Señor Preston did not happen."

"I think you took care of yourself very well against Preston," Carlos said. "The same goes for the trouble with Billings at the Cuero Quemado. What else are you looking for in the way of proof?"

"I do not know, Carlos. I am confused. I survived on the ranch near Kerrville, but my father couldn't stay away from the bottle. There was nothing I could do to save the ranch from going broke. Now here I am meeting other sorts of trouble. I just hate being a burden to anyone, especially you because I love you."

"Part of love is wanting to take care of the one you love," Carlos said. "You will be taking care of me and I will take care of you. It is not a matter of money either way. It is just how real love works."

"I suppose you are right. Perhaps I am expecting too much from myself."

"Maybe you are afraid of being a housebound wife with nothing else but cooking and cleaning to occupy your life. If that is what might be bothering you as far as us getting married, I will say that I would rather have you training young horses with your gentle hands than scrubbing floors and dirty clothes. I can hire someone to do that just as I do now. You are far too talented with horses to be doing things that we can pay to have done."

"You have never seen me train colts, Carlos."

"I have seen you ride and handle horses. I can see someone who is a part of the horse they are riding and not someone who sits in the saddle like a sack of wheat."

"When do you want to get married?" María asked.

"Are you saying you will marry me?"

"Yes, Carlos Montoya. I want to marry you with all my heart."

Carlos rose from his chair, pulled María up to stand next to him, and kissed her passionately. When he finally released her, he said, “I would like to marry you tonight, but I suppose we should wait until morning. I think we can marry with a judge rather than have to wait for the church to post bans and all that sort of thing. I am not very devout anyway, are you?”

“My mother was Catholic but Father was nothing that I know of. He never went to church. Actually my mother rarely attended church because we lived too far out in the country to get to town just for church on Sunday.”

“Tomorrow morning we will find a judge and by noon we will be Mister and Missus Carlos Montoya. Then I will tell Juan to stay at the corrals for three days.”

“Why? María asked, and laughed. They laughed together for a long moment.

After falling asleep fully clothed in each other’s arms, Carlos began to dream. He suddenly awakened and the dream stopped. He lay there without moving so as not to awaken María. *I wonder who that beautiful woman is whose body I could see through her robe. She let me feel her breasts and told me about love. Strange. I think I dreamed of her before*. He fell asleep again after thinking about the woman with the beautiful face and body that reminded him of María.

After breakfast. they dressed in their best clothes and walked to the building known as The Courthouse. Carlos had been there once before and was not comfortable to return, even for his wedding.

They went to the clerk’s office and Carlos paid for a marriage license. María stood next to him and smiled. Next, they followed the clerk's direction to the judge's chambers where they should find the judge because court was not in session that day. "Third door to the right," the clerk said. "The Judge's secretary will show you in."

"Thank you," Carlos said.

They walked out of the clerk's office and down the hall following the directions. Carlos knocked on the door. A man opened the door. "Can I help you?"

"Yes," Carlos said. "We are here to get married."

"Come with me," the old gray-haired secretary said as he turned his hunched over body around and led the way to the door to the judge's chambers.

The secretary opened the door after rapping once. "Your Honor, this couple is here to get married."

Carlos looked at the judge as he rose from his chair. He took Maria's arm. "I am sorry, I think we have come to the wrong place, Your Honor."

He turned making sure María was next to him and left the chambers. The secretary looked perplexed, but waited for them to leave before closing the door with the large shiny brass doorknob.

Carlos led María out of the courthouse and out onto the board sidewalk.

"What in the world was all that about? Are you suddenly afraid of getting married?"

"No, María. That is the Tejano judge from Mesilla who gave the San Ignacio de Toluca to Preston. I cannot allow that bribe taking mordilón to marry us. We will have to find another judge or some willing preacher. Maybe a preacher is the best answer. I do not trust anyone connected to what they call law around here. I do not want to take a chance that in a few years someone will knock on our door and say, 'so sorry, but you are not married. We have changed the rules'."

"I remember seeing a small building with a cross on top near where I bought the newspaper," María said.

"That is probably where we can get married without all the complicated religious procedure. That has to be the Reverend Foster's church. I think he calls himself Methodist. I hope he is home."

They arrived at the small church just off the main street of Rinconada and knocked on the door of the parsonage. A tall man with rusty red hair opened the door and asked what they were there for.

"We would like to have you marry us," Carlos said. "Here is our license."

"Come in," he said and looked at the license, "Ignacio and María. Have you both been baptized?"

"Yes," Carlos said, and nudged María.

"Yes," she said quickly.

"Do you have witnesses?"

"No," Carlos said.

"Well, you must find two witnesses because they have to sign your marriage certificate."

"Does it make any difference who the witnesses are?" Carlos asked.

"I suppose not, as long as they sign your certificate after the ceremony."

"All right," Carlos said. "We will be back shortly."

"Do I have to go, too?" María asked.

"You may stay here," Reverend Foster said. "That is, if it does not take long to find two witnesses."

"I know just where to find them quickly," Carlos said.

"Come, María, my wife is in the kitchen. You will enjoy her pleasant nature. She is a very God-fearing woman."

Carlos left to find the two witnesses. He hastened to the Glover Hotel Bar where the dilatants had gathered for their mid-morning refreshment.

Finding several Rinconadans at the bar he announced that he needed witnesses for his wedding and would pay two men a dollar each if they could spare ten minutes of their time. One man in denim work clothes and a partially smashed felt hat stood up, and another in clothes that looked like they belonged to a businessman, rose from his table. "When do we get paid?" the latter asked.

"When you have signed your name on the certificate," Carlos said.

The man flipped his right hand quickly up and down. "Count me in."

""For a dollar I would be happy to be your witness," the man in denim said.

"All right, let us get to the church as quickly as possible before my bride-to-be changes her mind," Carlos said and smiled at his takers.

Almost trotting back to the church building, Carlos led his witnesses, who he judged not drunk enough to ruin their role as those attesting to the legality of his marriage to María Penrose. The preacher opened the door to the church and beckoned Carlos in. María and the preacher's wife sat in the front pew.

Carlos led the witnesses to the front of the church, a distance of less than twenty feet.

Foster gave instructions to all. He positioned the witnesses in the front row of pews, had his wife act as bride's maid, and began the ceremony. "We are gathered together..." When he came to the part where the bride and groom had to repeat after him they looked at each other with love in their eyes. Then the reverend said, "With this ring I thee wed" for Carlos to repeat. A surprised look came on Carlos's face and his eyebrows raised above the twinkle in his eyes.

"We did not think about the ring, Reverend," Carlos said. "Is it possible to do all this without a ring?"

Foster pondered the question for a moment before looking in his wife's direction. "Lillian, would you please take off your wedding ring and lend it to Mister Montoya?"

"Of course, Rufus," she said. "I would be happy to lend it for the ceremony."

Lillian removed her wedding band and took it to Carlos.

"With this ring I thee wed," Carlos said and put it on Maria's finger. The ring proved to be close to Maria's size but a fraction too small. María took hold of the ring and pushed it on.

Rufus Foster then pronounced them husband and wife and told Carlos he could kiss the bride.

The Reverend Foster's service did not take long, even with the pause concerning the ring. Carlos kissed María. The witnesses signed the license, took the two dollars from Carlos and left to return to the Glover Bar. Carlos paid Foster two dollars and María tried to remove the ring to return it to the preacher's wife. It would not pass over her knuckle; try as she did to wiggle it over it. "I cannot seem to get the ring off," she said.

"Come with me, dear" Lillian said. "I'll put soap on your finger and the ring should slide off."

María followed Lillian through the door to the parsonage. Carlos stood patiently waiting with the preacher. "I understand you trade horses and mules and maintain a livery stable. Is that right, Mister Montoya?"

"Yes. María will be helping train the young horses."

"Are you planning to raise a family?" Foster asked.

"I have not given much thought to that, Reverend."

"Perhaps you should stop by so we can talk about God's plan," Foster said.

Before Carlos could think of an answer, María returned with the preacher's wife. They had successfully removed the ring.

"Now you must find a ring for her to wear, Mister Montoya," Lillian said. "She is a married woman now."

"Yes, Missus Foster. I will tend to that right away," Carlos said and turned to María who had a impish grin on her face. "Shall we go?"

"Yes, and thank you so much for the use of your ring, Missus Foster," María said.

"Think nothing of it. It was my pleasure."

Carlos and María made their exit as quickly as possible. Once out of hearing distance, Carlos glanced back, then continued toward the center of town. "I am glad that is over," he said. "That preacher is very intrusive. He asked me if we were planning to raise a family. I would say that it is none of his business."

"Do not be angry with the poor man." María said. "Think about how he feels. He must live the life of a man of God. I am so happy that you and I are the way we are."

"I am, too."

They passed in front of a store that sold jewelry and sundries. "Perhaps we should go into Morgan's right now and buy a ring," Carlos said.

"That was so funny when the preacher said to repeat after him, 'with this ring I thee wed,' and you did not have a ring to wed me with. We might have thought this out further, but I am glad we did not," María said.

They went into the store and approached the jewelry counter. The clerk strolled over and stood behind the counter for a moment. "Do you see anything you like, Mister Montoya?" he asked

"We are looking for a wedding band," Carlos said.

The clerk brought out a tray of gold and silver bands and put it on top of the counter. María tried several on and found one that she liked and also fit.

"I like this one, Carlos."

"Good. That was quick."

He paid for the band, which she put on her finger. "I will make believe we had this one all the time," she said when they had left the store.

Before returning to the house they visited Juan at the corrals to tell him about getting married. While there, Carlos showed María the three colts he had bought to train for saddle horses. They were all two-year-olds and all three had been gelded. Two were brown and the third dappled gray. The gray stood slightly taller than the browns and had a wary look in his eye.

"The gray might prove to be a handful," María said. "He has that certain look that some horses have. I will have to pay more attention to that fellow than to the others or I might get sent flying half way to the moon."

"I told you that you knew horses," Carlos said. "I think you have the gray figured very well. However, I know you will have him gentled in a short time and we can sell him for a reliable saddle horse even before he is a three-year-old."

Juan was not surprised at the news of their marriage. Carlos took him aside and asked him to stay in the barn for a couple of nights. Juan grinned and told Carlos that he should get a room at the Glover.

"I would if I thought I would not run into Preston. If he made one remark to María, I would have him swallowing my fist and that is not what my mood is right now."

"I know what your mood is, Brother," Juan said, and his grin entirely covered his face.

Leaving the corrals Carlos suggested they have an early supper at the Black Bull Café. The place had gained instant popularity since it had opened a year ago among cattlemen and horsemen from around Rinconada. Carlos seldom ate there because the work at the corrals took up most of his waking hours.

They enjoyed their supper and being together. Carlos changed the subject of their conversation from training the colts to whether or not they should remain in Rinconada where there seemed to be a potential threat from Preston and the ever present concern about the Apache raiders.

"I do not think Señor Preston will bother me since he discovered that I am half Mexican," María said. "I will bet he finds himself a gringa soon."

"The Apaches are bound to continue raiding until the army puts a stop to their activities," Carlos said. "I must take my turns at the barn at night in case they decide to steal our horses. It is too bad they do not prefer rattlesnake over horsemeat."

"What do you suggest we do?" María asked.

"I have thought for some time that Mexico might be a place of opportunity for those of us who were Mexican before the Gadsden Purchase and still feel Mexican in spite of the change in citizenship. I am not happy with the way the Tejanos regard us."

After finishing their dessert of flan, they left for their wedding night in the house on Calle Principal. Carlos made sure the doors had been secured and went into his bedroom to wait for María.

Much to his surprise, María walked into his room completely nude and stood in the doorway smiling. He stared at her beauty for a moment before beginning to undress himself. “I cannot believe how beautiful you are, María,” he said, dropping his trousers on the floor of the bedroom.

He stepped over to her, put his arms around her waist and kissed her slowly and fervently. “I feel like I have wanted you forever,” he said when he had released her lips.

“I feel the same way, Carlos. I love you with all my heart. I am so very happy to be your wife.”

They stepped over to the bed and followed whatever came into their minds until first morning light when they slipped into peaceful slumber in each other’s arms.

CHAPTER TWELVE

Carlos bought a double bed for the room in the barn. Whenever it was his turn to guard the corral he and María slept in the room together. One morning, a month after the wedding, soon after waking up during their turn at guard, María had gone out to the corral to look at the gray colt. Carlos checked a harness in need of repair that he had bought along with a team of buggy horses.

Suddenly María came running around the side of the barn. "Come quickly," she said. "I think we have unwelcome visitors. I was just about to ride the gray when I thought I saw someone outside the corral."

Carlos dropped the harness and his needle onto the table and followed his wife around the barn to the corrals. María ducked down and motioned Carlos to do the same as they rushed down the alley between the pens. Arriving at the large corral, she opened the gate and, still crouching, made her way to the outer side of the estacada built structure. Standing up she pointed across the river.

"Look," she said. "They are about to go into the bosque."

"They are Apache all right," Carlos said. "See their buckskins and headbands. Just two of them probably means they are scouting to see what they have to do to get to the horses to steal them."

"I saw movement on the outside between the mesquite poles that are stacked. I knew it must be someone who did not wish to be seen by the way they crouched."

"I wonder if they noticed the alarm wire that goes along the top through the screw eyes."

"When I saw them they were not looking over the top of the corral. They seemed to be looking between the mesquite poles."

"Even if they saw the wire, the chances are that they would not realize that it is an alarm. We need to tell Juan about this when he finishes breakfast and comes to work. I would almost put money on the Apache attempting to steal from our corral. It will not be tonight or tomorrow, but it might be. ¿Quien sabe"

"Should we get some help?" María asked.

"We might have to have help waiting for a month," Carlos said. "The best thing to do is make sure the alarm is working every night before we go to bed. I do not expect them to try stealing from us in daylight. They do not like to fight a battle at night but I think they are not above stealing."

"As you explained to me once before, they are just shopping for groceries," María said.

"Tonight is a new moon. I doubt if they will try until there is more moonlight."

"You seem to know them quite well," she said.

"I wish I knew them better. What they did to my parents and sister was terrible. I will never be able to chase that out of my mind."

"I suppose we all have demons to deal with," she said. "Do you think it is safe to go back to what I was about to do and ride the gray?"

"I cannot see any danger today. But, keep an eye out. Those devils are not very predictable. Besides, Juan and I will be here."

Carlos watched María return to ride the gray colt, quietly teaching him what the reins were meant for. She worked the colt with steady, light hands, talking to him as if he were human.

Carlos went back to repairing the harness as Juan arrived for the day's work. Carlos explained about the Apache scouting party and they both searched their minds for a plan to repel the raiders should they make an attempt to steal horses. "Maybe we should both stand guard for a while," Juan said. "We can take turns staying awake to make sure they do not sneak in without setting off our alarm."

"If we follow our original plan we can probably scare them away with a few shots from our carbines," Carlos said. "They will not expect that."

"You are probably right," Juan replied." I hope you are right."

"Just make sure we shoot to kill," Carlos said. "That is the only language they will understand."

"I wonder how many times they have scouted our corrals," Juan said.

"There is no telling. We know they came today and that is enough to get our worrying going. Before you go to bed tonight, make sure you test the alarm. In fact, it might be a good idea to test it while I am still here to listen inside the room."

Before Carlos and María started for the house on Calle Principal, Carlos sat on the bed in the sleeping room of the barn as Juan went around disturbing the wire, that when moved, rang a small cow bell in the room. When they had first installed the device, they had tested it to determine if the bell could be heard outside the barn. The sound remained inside the room. The bell rang several times as Juan walked along the corrals snapping the wire as someone might if they were climbing over the mesquite poles stacked between the double posts.

The following morning Carlos felt happy that the alarm had not sounded and nobody, Apaches or just plain horse thieves, had attempted a robbery. They continued to be wary, and each evening, for two weeks, they tested the device.

The moon had filled out and gave enough light so that anyone could easily see where he or she wanted to go. Carlos and María took their turn on guard. Standing his carbine by the door to the room, Carlos went to bed with María in his arms. "Suppose the bell rings?" she asked. "Do you plan to climb the ladder to the barn window as naked as you are right now?"

"I just hope the bell does not ring until I finish what is on my mind," he said, and laughed.

A half hour later he rose and got dressed before going back to bed and sleep. He had barely closed his eyes when the bell began tinkling in an uneven rhythm. Carlos threw off the covers, jammed on his boots and grabbed his carbine as he left the room to head for the ladder.

Climbing quickly to the top, he peered out the window surveying the corrals. He could not see any movement, even among the horses that stood in silence with the night. Suddenly he saw what was causing the bell to ring. There on the top of the corral in which María had been riding the colts, his eyes darted quickly to the sound of two cats mating in the moonlight. Climbing back down the ladder, he returned to the room and slipped into bed next to María.

"What was it?" she asked.

"A pair of cats making kittens," he said, and laughed. "I guess that means the wire is sensitive enough."

"I am glad it was cats and not an Apache raiding party."

"I share that, but it is a perfect night for the Apache. Once the cats have accomplished what they came for, I still must answer to the sound of the bell."

The bell awakened Carlos again just before first morning light. Again, he pulled on his boots and climbed the ladder with his carbine to look out of the window.

The four Apache men had taken several of the mesquite poles from one of the sections. Carlos waited and watched as they worked to dismantle the corral in order to steal the three colts that had backed into the north corner sensing something was wrong. Just as one of the Indians reached up for another pole, Carlos aimed and fired his carbine. He heard the thunk of the bullet striking and entering the man's side. The Indian fell off the corral, landing on the outside. Spotting another Indian with a rifle, Carlos aimed and fired again. The second victim sprawled on the ground and ceased moving.

Carlos remained on the ladder to watch what they might do next. Certainly with two either dead or badly wounded they would not try to complete the robbery.

María, fully clothed, appeared at the bottom of the ladder. “Are they still here?” she said in a whisper.

Carlos turned and nodded his head affirmatively.

“Did you hit any?”

Again he turned and held up two fingers.

Carlos watched as the two who had not been in his line of fire, quickly carried the other two away from the corral, not wanting to become victims of the rifle fire that must have seemed to them to be coming from the sky. That is what Carlos thought. He also thought he had done well in protecting the horses. He remained looking out of the window. In moments he heard hoof beats as the Indians made their way across the river’s floodplain in the moonlight. Carlos saw them in the distance as they broke out of the bosque heading for the distant mountains, where they would tend to their dead or wounded. Carlos would never know, nor did he care to know.

Climbing down the ladder, he took María into his arms. “Well, my love, we need to go and make sure those colts do not try jumping out of the corral. In fact, we should put them in another corral and fix theirs in the morning when we can see,”

They took halters into the corral and approached the colts. The intruding Indians and the rifle fire had spooked them badly. At first the horses backed away from Carlos and María even though they were familiar people to them.

Catching them finally, they led the colts out of the corral and into another that held four saddle horses that had arrived with some travelers.

The colts stuck together and trotted to an empty corner. Carlos and María returned to their room. "Should we get naked again, or do you think the Apache raiders are still hungry?" María asked, and smiled.

"For a woman who was chaste until her wedding night, you certainly have learned a lot," Carlos said.

"Who taught me, Carlos Montoya?"

Carlos told Juan about the Apache visitors when he arrived at the corrals after breakfast. They went out to inspect the damage and repaired the section in a few minutes, taking care to make sure the wire alarm system was back in working order. Carlos and María rode back to the house for their breakfast.

They enjoyed chatting about the episode of the raiders, and agreed that they needed to be diligent in their efforts to detect any more attempts by the Apache and others as well. With the drought affecting everything in the territory, bandits were tempted to steal horses and mules that were not guarded by their owners.

Two weeks passed with no further trouble from the Indians. Then, the news spread quickly that the other livery stable had been cleaned out of every animal, including a jackass that they used to breed mares to get mules. The Hungerford family had lost everything but their land, corrals, tack, and what grain and hay was in the barn.

Carlos rode across town to see Tom Hungerford and offer any help he could, but Hungerford turned to him in anger. “You goddamn Mex, you have nearly put me out of business since you started your livery,” Hungerford said. “I don’t need your kind of help so why don’t you just ride the hell out of here and leave me to my business.”

Carlos reined the bay gelding around without another word. He had heard enough and hoped he would never meet Tom Hungerford anywhere. Another Tejano cabrón.

A week after his confrontation with Hungerford, Carlos and María headed for the house on Calle Principal for breakfast after spending the night together on their turn at guard duty in the room in the barn.

Arriving at the house they found an envelope inserted into the brass handle of the front door. Carlos took it and opened it. Will Barlow of The Territorial Bank had written a short note. “Barlow, the banker, wants to see me,” Carlos said. “I wonder why. I do not owe him any money.”

“Maybe he heard about your alarm system and wants to be partners with you,” María said.

“I never told anyone about that alarm system because you never know who might want to know. I did not tell anyone about the Apache visit either.”

“It sounds to me that if you want to know what the banker has in mind you need to go to the bank and ask him,” María said.

“I will ride over to the bank after breakfast. What are we having this fine morning in October?”

“I thought chorizo con huevos might take the chill out of our bones.”

“That sounds absolutely wonderful.”

“It certainly does, but there is a slight problem,” María said.

“And, what is the problem?” Carlos asked with his arms folded in front of him and cocking his head to one side.

“We do not have any chorizo,” María said with her head cocked the same way. “But we do have some great frijoles. I will fry them in lard and add a little cheese to make you think you are having a treat.”

Carlos laughed at Maria’s humor. “There is never a dull moment living with you, María Montoya.”

After breakfast, Carlos rode to town and tethered the bay gelding to the bank’s hitch rail. The front door was closed, but Will Barlow saw Carlos and rose from his desk to go to the door and unlock it. “Come in, Carlos,” the banker said. “I take it you found my note?”

Yes, Mister Barlow,” Carlos answered. “I am curious why you want to see me since I do not think I owe you any money.”

“Oh, I know you don’t owe a dime. I wanted to talk to you about The Hungerford Livery. I am sure you have heard the news about the Apache raiding party that cleaned him out.”

“As a matter of fact I did, and I rode over there to ask Hungerford if I could be of help in some way. He called me a goddamn Mex and did not want any help from me, so I rode away.”

"That is unfortunate. Hungerford could use all the help he can get, but what I want to talk to you about is your possible interest in buying out Hungerford Livery."

"I am sorry to disappoint you, Mister Barlow, but I do not want any further dealings with that Tejano."

"You don't have to deal with Hungerford. The Territorial Bank now owns the land and improvements of Hungerford Livery. You will deal only with me."

"Why would I want to buy a livery that is broke when I have one that is doing a good job of making us a living?"

"I suggest that the opportunity to expand your business might prove lucrative."

"Tell me what you mean by lucrative. My English is fair, but that is a word I don't know."

"By lucrative I mean that you might be able to make money by owning the only two livery stables in town."

"Mister Barlow, let us put all the cards on the table," Carlos said. "Hungerford owed you money. When the Apache raiders wiped him out he can no longer pay his loan so the bank took his land and corrals. Now, you are trying to sell me the land and the corrals because you, as a banker do not wish to be in the livery business. Is that correct?"

"I think you have it very well figured out, Carlos. Are you interested in expanding?"

"I might be, depending on what is involved."

"I can sell you the land and improvements of Hungerford Livery for two thousand dollars."

"That does sound reasonable, but I do not want to own land that you Americans can take away from me in the court house like they did with Toluca. I owned land that the Americans now own. I never sold it. The judge hammered his gavel and then Preston owned my land. I will not let that happen to me again. I hope you understand."

"So you are interested?"

"I am interested, but I would like to rent the property rather than buy it. You see, Mister Barlow, I have no trust in your legal system. I rent the corrals where we are now. I even rent our house."

"I am aware of that," Barlow said. "How much rent are you willing to pay for Hungerford Livery?"

"I must talk that over with my brother," Carlos said. "How much rent are you asking?"

"I haven't thought about renting the property. I would rather sell it."

"As I said, Mister Barlow, I do not want to own anything that can be taken away from me so easily as was San Ignacio de Toluca."

"Have a talk with your brother and let me know what you decide. I promise I will not act on this further until I hear from you."

"Fair enough. I can have an answer by this afternoon."

"I look forward to seeing you later today."

Juan had just finished harnessing a team of horses to a buckboard when Carlos arrived at the corrals. The customer helped his wife to the seat and walked around to take his place. Juan handed the man the reins and walked over to the barn where Carlos had dismounted and was loosening the cinch on his saddle. “María said you had gone to the bank,” Juan said. “What for?”

“Barlow sent me a note that he wanted to see me,” Carlos replied. “He wants to sell us the Hungerford Livery because that Apache raid wiped them out and they went under. Barlow now owns the livery.”

“He does not own much,” Juan said. “I rode by there the other day and it is a wonder that the horses they did have stayed in the corrals. There is not one corral in the entire livery that does not need a major amount of repair.”

“I saw that, too,” Carlos said. “I told Barlow we do not want to buy the livery but might rent it from him. Barlow tried to tell me that by having the Hungerford livery we would eliminate competition. I have never seen Hungerford as a competitor. We get customers from the Paso del Norte road as well as the one from Sonora.”

“If we had both liveries we would have to hire guards instead of doing that ourselves,” Juan said.

“To eliminate the competition,” Carlos replied, and then laughed as he remembered Barlow’s advice about competition. “Barlow tried to scare me with competition to try and sell me the livery. I wonder how many places Barlow has foreclosed on during this drought. He seemed very anxious for me to take that livery off his hands. It might be a good time to teach him that we Mexicans are not stupid.”

Carlos turned toward the gate as Captain Tillinghast rode through into the barnyard. He reined in his horse at the hitch rail and dismounted stiffly. “Well, Montoya, how is life treating you?”

“Very well, Captain. How are those mules I bought for you turning out?”

The mules are doing quite well. In fact the colonel sent me to town to see if you can find more mules to buy. It seems that when the general came by last week, he saw the mules and wants thirty of them.”

“My man has about twelve left but they are the mules I cut back for one reason or another. I would have to look around and see if I could find more. This drought might make people want to sell to save grass, but finding the quality I did before is going to take a lot of riding.”

“I suppose you will want a deposit,” Tillinghast said.

“I haven’t changed my way of doing business, Captain.”

“Very well, I will inform the colonel about the situation and see what his decision will be.”

“We will be here,” Carlos said.

The captain mounted his horse and left without further conversation.

“I do not think the captain likes me,” Carlos said.

“I must agree with you, Brother. When are you going back to see Barlow?”

“I told him I will have an answer for him this afternoon.”

Carlos arrived at The Territorial Bank just before closing time. Barlow rose from his chair as Carlos walked over to his desk. Barlow extended his hand. Carlos took it and the two greeted each other with smiles. "Well, what did your brother, Juan, think about the expansion plan?" Barlow asked.

"Neither of us feel that we should have our money tied up in a piece of property. We need to have trading money."

"You can always borrow from the bank. I consider you good customers with excellent credit."

"We both appreciate that, but we are now in a position where we do not have to borrow and pay interest. Instead you pay us interest."

"I can understand that."

"You see, with the Hungerford place we would have to hire guards since we must stay at our place to make sure Apaches do not come again. You may not have heard that we had a raiding party a while back and I was able to chase them off with two well placed shots from my carbine."

"I can't say that I did hear about that. The only raid I know about is the one that wiped out Hungerford."

"Also, Juan and I know that the Hungerford place needs a lot of repair before it can be used for our business. I am sure that the condition of those corrals had a lot to do with the reason Hungerford' business was not doing well before the raid. Not many people would want their horses kept in falling apart corrals."

"I have seen that condition also. However, I cannot afford to pay for those repairs because I have had to foreclose on too many properties in the past six months. This drought is taking a real toll."

"I am sorry we cannot help you with the Hungerford place. You have been good to us and we appreciate it.," Carlos said, and rose from his chair to leave. Before turning toward the door, he raised his right hand slightly. "Mister Barlow, I may need our money in the next day or so if the Army wants me to ride south for more mules."

"Just let me know," Barlow said, and returned to the papers he had on the top of his desk.

María had finished riding all three colts and Juan had started feeding when Carlos returned from the bank.

"Juan told me about the Hungerford Livery deal," María said. "What happened?"

Juan came to the barn with a pitchfork in his hand.

"I told Mister Barlow that we were not interested," Carlos said. "I also told him I would be needing the money we have on deposit if the Army wants more mules."

"It sounds to me like we are making more progress than we had hoped for," Juan said.

"I am concerned about getting thirty more mules for Captain Tillinghast. The twelve Alvarez mules I cut back are probably not worth looking at and I do not know anyone else down in Sonora who raises mules."

"If you go riding down there just looking around, you might be wasting your time and horseshoes," María said.

"I have been thinking that I should refuse the order because of the scarcity of mules that can't be bought at a price that we can make money on."

"That makes more sense than going on a wild chase after something that does not exist," María said.

Just as Carlos saddled the bay for the ride to the bank, Captain Tillinghast rode up to the hitch rail and dismounted. "Well, Montoya, the colonel sent me back to ask you to buy thirty more mules. However, he is somewhat upset that you continue to require a deposit."

"Tell the colonel that I no longer require a deposit," Carlos said as he tightened the cinch on his saddle.

"He will be pleased," Tillinghast said.

"I doubt it. I do not want a deposit because I am not going to try to fill the order."

"Why not?"

"Because, Captain, I do not know where to look for any more mules of that quality."

"The colonel will be quite disappointed, I am sure."

"That I cannot help," Carlos said. "I must leave now as I have business to take care of."

He mounted the bay and booted him into a trot toward Washington Street, never looking back at the captain whose manner and attitude he had come to dislike. He felt a pleasant relief having turned down the order for the mules.

Carlos went to the bank to tell Mister Barlow that he would not need any money to buy mules for the army. They chatted about what had happened with Toluca.

"Perhaps if I had known more English, Señor Preston could not have taken away San Ignacio de Toluca from us."

"That is difficult to say one way or another," Barlow said. "Speaking of Steve Preston, I wonder if you might be available to do something for me. Of course I will pay you for your trouble."

"Wait a minute, Mister Barlow," Carlos interrupted. "I have no desire to confront Preston in any way."

"You won't have to see him unless he sees you first. What I need you to do is ride out and inspect your old place and come back with your observations as to the condition of the cattle and the rangeland."

"Why me, Mister Barlow?"

"You know what the place looked like when you left it. Preston has asked for an additional loan and I need to know what you think of the way he is managing things there."

"I am not sure if my opinion will help. I am sure I do not agree with the way Preston is managing Toluca because I know for a fact that he has put too many steers on the range."

"I will pay you twenty dollars to ride out there and tell me what is going on," Barlow said.

Carlos hesitated a few moments, trying to decide if he wanted to get involved with the request. "There is one covenant we need to make," Carlos said and smiled. "Señor Preston must not know about this."

"You have my word on it. I am not a judge of ranch land and you are. That is why I need your opinion. Nobody is better qualified to judge than you."

"How soon do you need to know?"

"Preston said he would be in town next Friday. That gives you three days. Is that enough? If not I can stall him for a week."

"I will ride out there tomorrow and return the following day. That should give me enough time to see what is going on."

"That seems fine," Barlow said.

"Thank you, Mister Barlow. I will see you the day after tomorrow with my opinion of Toluca."

"I appreciate you agreeing to do this for me," Barlow said.

Carlos left the bank and returned to the corrals. He told Juan and Maria about the inspection job for Barlow that he had contracted for.

"Just watch out that Señor Preston does not discover what you are doing," María said.

"If I meet anyone on this ride, I plan to tell them I am traveling through to go hunting in the mountains. I will have a pack horse so hunting will be believable."

"When will you leave," María asked.

"Tomorrow morning before sunrise. I will spend the night and ride back the next day. Barlow said that Preston plans on being in town on Friday. It looks like he has not changed any of his habits."

The early morning chill made Carlos shiver as he put on his jacket and left for the corrals. Juan still slept in the barn room, so Carlos took care in being as quiet as possible getting the bay saddled and the sorrel pack horse loaded with his bedding and what little food he though he would need for the two days.

Once ready, he wasted no time and left Rinconada at a trot, fast enough to cover a lot of ground in a short time and slow enough not to tire the horses. By noon he had entered Toluca range. He had not ventured there since getting Maria's cameo and clothes, so the sight of grasses grazed down to their roots saddened him. The first waterhole he went to was called Borrego Tank. He remembered his grandfather telling about making the reservoir with teams of mules hitched to fresnos, iron scrapers that dug the hole to catch runoff water from an arroyo. One of the first animals Ysidoro saw besides cattle was a mountain sheep that had migrated to the flatlands. So he had named the tank Borrego after the sheep. Carlos looked at the dry, caked silt at the bottom of the tank. It must have been dry for three months. Around the tank, the grasses had been entirely cropped off and bare dirt remained. Under a mesquite tree he spotted the bones of a dead cow, her hide dried and brittle being eaten away by bugs of several varieties. Her flesh had been devoured by buzzards and coyotes months before.

He rode around the area and saw three more bone piles that looked like Texas steers judging from the horns on the skulls. He sat in the saddle looking at what to him had become a tragic sight. Wondering what the rest of the ranch looked like, he began riding again, heading toward the mountain country in case someone rode up on him and questioned what he was doing on Toluca.

The next tank he came to, Agua Zarca, looked like Borrego but there were more bones around it. The evidence pointed to poor management. Had the Preston crew ridden diligently as the waterholes began to dry up they could have moved the cattle and possibly saved their lives. Then he thought about the naked range and wondered if they would have starved to death anyway.

By evening he had seen enough to form an opinion that Barlow should use to reject Preston's loan application. Carlos decided that any further riding would not add to his thoughts. Instead of making camp and spending the night, he turned back toward Rinconada. Riding through the night did not bother him except for the chill. But, he had done it many times before. The thought of sliding into bed next to María gave him all the incentive he needed to keep the horses moving toward home.

Putting the horses in the small corral behind the house, he slipped into the kitchen and began undressing.

"Who is there?" Maria's voice sounded from the bedroom.

"Me, Carlos. I could not stand to be away from you."

"What time is it?" she asked.

"The clock in the kitchen says it is three in the morning."

He finished undressing and went to the bedroom. Crawling in beside his wife, he took her into his arms. "You are so wonderful to be with," he said. "I put two tired horses in the corral."

“I am glad you came home early, Carlos. I thought about you all day long. What did you find out?”

“The place is a barren waste and there are more dead carcasses than I ever imagined. I do not want to see that again.”

He caressed her and kissed her willing lips. His thoughts about Toluca vanished.

CHAPTER THIRTEEN

The banker listened intently to Carlos's report. A distinct scowl made his eyebrows lower to begin pushing against his eyelids. His right hand covered his mouth. Carlos finished by saying that he was shocked at the condition of the range.

"We had drought before but we sold off cattle rather than adding more. From what I have heard, these Tejanos ruined their range so they came here. Now they are ruining this range. They did not learn anything."

"I have heard the same story from others, and from what you say about Preston's management, the story sounds valid. Thank you for your efforts and here, take this."

Barlow handed Carlos a twenty dollar gold piece, which he slipped into his pocket. "Thank you, Mister Barlow. I wish I could have brought back a better report."

"What you brought back is the information I need to make an intelligent decision, in the matter of a loan to Preston."

Carlos went to the Hotel Glover bar and ordered a mescal. Guillermo Gallegos stood next to him. Carlos had known Guillermo since they were young and Guillermo had joined in the gathers. They greeted one another and lifted their glasses.

"How are your cattle holding up during this drought, Memo?"

"They are pretty thin, but I put them in the mountains where some of the springs are still trickling."

"I guess there are some ranchers who have lost a lot," Carlos said.

"Some of them deserve to lose everything. That Tejano cabrón Preston, who got your place, brought in a bunch of Texas steers and I will bet that most of them are white, bleached bones by now."

"I heard about that," Carlos said. "What are two and three-year-old steers bringing these days?"

"If you can find a buyer, you might get fifty cents. The cattle are worth little but their hides, and the hides are in bad shape."

Carlos and Gallegos chatted through another drink. Carlos left the bar and headed home. At supper Carlos brought up the old plan the Montoya brothers had when they first left the ranch. María listened.

"Juan," Carlos said. "I think we should not think about stealing those steers if there are any left. Guillermo Gallegos told me today that if we could find a buyer the steer might bring fifty cents a head. I say that is not enough to risk getting caught. And, even if we did not get caught, we could not sell the steers."

"I have to agree with you. I will go to see Pedro tomorrow and tell him what we are thinking just in case he is still thinking about the revenge."

"Revenge is not useful," Carlos said.

"I agree one hundred percent," María said.

Juan left for the corral guard duty.

"I remember a dream I had a while ago," Carlos said.

"We were driving eight hundred steers crossing some big river and all of a sudden a giant whirlpool swallowed up all the steers."

"That must have been quite a dream," María said. "Every once in a while I remember some dream I have had. They are weird."

"I have told you that I think I met you in a dream before I met you at the ranch."

"I know. That is weird, too. All I know is I love you with or without your dreams," María said.

"I am glad," Carlos said, and rose from the chair to lead her into the bedroom.

A month passed quickly in spite of winter. A few winter storms came through, but they did not yield enough rainfall to break the drought. The horse and mule business continued to make a good living for Carlos, María and Juan.

The three colts that María had trained turned out to be excellent saddle horses and commanded top dollar. The man who bought the gray left him with María to see if she could train him to race.

Carlos bought three more two-year-olds and María started them as soon as they arrived. Teams of horses and mules held up in price in spite of the drought. Carlos found a ready market for them with the farmers who began to break ground along one of the tributaries of the river. The Apaches posed a constant problem for them, but the farmers soon got used to keeping their horses and mules under guard at night.

Another note from Barlow came toward the end of April. The banker wanted to see Carlos as soon as possible. At the supper table the conversation centered around the Hungerford Livery lease because all three thought that was what the banker wanted to talk about.

The following morning, Carlos showed up at the bank just before it opened. Barlow hurried to the door, unlocked it, and let him in. "Good morning, Carlos," he said. "It is nice of you to come so soon."

"You said in your note 'as soon as possible'. I read the note last night after you had closed. This is as soon as possible."

They sat down by the desk. "What I wanted to talk to you about is The San Ignacio de Toluca. As I am sure you remember, I sent you out there to tell me what the conditions were. Your report helped me a great deal in making my decision not to loan Steve Preston any more money. I have just finished foreclosing on the ranch and the cattle."

"I do not think you foreclosed on much, Mister Barlow."

"I haven't even been out there because I wouldn't know what I was looking at. Since the bank now owns Toluca and its cattle, I am in a position to make you an offer if you would like to buy your old ranch back."

"Mister Barlow, I appreciate your consideration. However, I have no desire to buy Toluca back. Remember I rode out there and it is now a barren wasteland. I would wager that the number of cattle still left would surprise you, especially if you looked at your books and saw how many Preston claimed when he borrowed your money on them."

"You will only pay for the cattle that are there now," Barlow said.

"I have given a lot of thought about what I am doing now. We are trading horses and mules and my wife is having a wonderful time training colts with her gentle hands. You know, Mister Barlow, when I ranched Toluca I worked from before sunrise until after darkness most of the time. It was tough work and then there was the weather to deal with. I had absolutely no control over the weather. If it rained I had feed for the cattle. If it did not rain I had to sell off cattle I was not ready to sell."

"But you were a successful rancher, Carlos."

"Because I worked. Then, in spite of all that, a Tejano comes along and takes over Toluca because the deed had burned in a fire in Arispe many years ago. Even now when I think about what happened, my anger comes close to making me vomit. Why should I buy something that was stolen from me in the first place? Of course you would not consider giving it back as the return of stolen property."

"I'll tell you what, Carlos. I will sell you Toluca for four thousand dollars and you can pay me after you sell your first calf crop. I will sell the cattle for a dollar a head. I will still be losing money. I shouldn't have loaned Preston a dime."

"Where is Preston now?"

"I hired him to care take the ranch until I sell it. He says he will go back to Texas when I sell it."

"I have to tell you something, Mister Barlow, but first I would like to ask where you came from?"

"Philadelphia," the banker said.

"I do not even know where that is, but I am from here. When your Mister Gadsden bought this land from Mexico, they said I had become an American. I did not know what I was because I had always been a Mexican and I was happy being a Mexican. Then the Tejanos began coming here. They referred to us as Mexes and greasers, yet we were supposed to be Americans. I have watched the Tejanos, especially that bastard Preston who beat my wife. He is a coward and a thieving mordilón. He ruined a good ranch and now is going back to Texas where he belongs. Mister Barlow, I belong here. This is where I was born and raised. This is my country, whether I am called a Mex or an American. You are from somewhere else, but it was, I assume, part of America. Yet you are not used to the business of raising cattle and horses. I am sorry you are losing money, but I cannot help that.

"What about my offer, Carlos?"

"I do not want to own any land here. I once did and it was stolen from me. I am afraid I have little trust left in your system. I will make my way my own way with my own livery stable"

"Well, I am sorry I can't interest you in Toluca.

Carlos rose from the chair. His back felt sweaty from the tensions of the conversation. He left the bank and went back to the corrals where María and Juan would be working. He told them about his conversation with Barlow.

"From what you said about the ranch, I think you made a good choice by refusing his offer," María said. "I think we are doing well right here and I must say I am happier than I have ever been in my entire life."

"I agree with María, Brother. We do not need to take back a place that will be a burden instead of an asset."

"I also went further and told Barlow that I was once very confused about where I belonged after the Gadsden deal. I do not feel that way now. I belong here. This is my land to live on no matter what flag is flying over the town. The Tejanos do not belong here as much as I do. They can call me a Mex or a greaser all they want, but I belong here. They do not.

Just as he finished talking, Steve Preston rode up to the hitch rail and dismounted. Carlos looked at María and then to Juan. All three shrugged at Preston's unexpected arrival, and María walked into the barn.

He strode over with his thumbs sticking in behind his belt.

"Montoya, I came over to see if we could make bygones be bygones."

"I cannot see why not," Carlos said. "Do you have something on your mind?"

"As a matter of fact I do," Preston said. "I must go back to Kerrville. I have a lot to do back there on some ranches I own so I would like to sell San Ignacio de Toluca and the cattle back to you."

This man has absolutely no truth to him. "How much are you asking?" Carlos asked.

“Well, I figure the ranch is worth five thousand and the cattle, since they are all well located, are worth two dollars a head. That’s less than I paid you for them. I’ll throw in the mares and stallion.”

“I find this interesting, Señor Preston. You stole my ranch through a questionable deal and now you want to sell it back to me after you have put too many cattle on it and they have eaten all the grass like a barber can shave the whiskers off a sixteen year old’s cheek.”

“I’ve had a drought to reckon with, Montoya.”

“I am very aware of the drought. Let me say this, Preston. If I did want to buy Toluca back, I would buy it from Mister Barlow. His offer was better than yours. You stole a good ranch, mistreated it so badly that it isn’t even worth stealing now. You probably did me a favor in the long run. When I worked the San Ignacio de Toluca range when it was Mexico I had drought and cattle prices to deal with. After your railroad builder, Gadsden disenfranchised us of our land and our citizenship as Mexicans, my brothers and I licked our wounds and began our lives again. We have a successful business that is not dependent upon the rain and the price of steers. And, it was you who brought the most wonderful woman I have ever known out to New Mexico Territory, and now she is my wife. I suppose I have lots to thank you for even if you are a goddamn Tejano. Now, if you will excuse me, we Americans have a business to attend to.

Carlos watched as Preston returned to the hitch rail, grabbed the reins and mounted his horse. Then Carlos turned and went to the barn where María waited.

“María”, Carlos said, once inside and standing by the bench where she sat. “Just now, expressing my deep anger toward Preston as I talked to him has cleansed me of those vengeful feelings I have had since I lost Toluca. I once thought I owed it to my grandfather to get Toluca back in the Montoya name, and I had no idea how to do that. Now I realize that my grandfather never would have asked that. I now understand what happened to clear my mind of so much self-pity and guilt. Now, I can live my life with a sense of peace within myself even though it will take time to feel like I belong here in the land that was once a part of Mexico. One of those dreams was about you.” He reached down for her hands. She stood up and went into his arms.

“I will always love you, María.”

* * * END * * *

ABOUT THE AUTHOR

John Duncklee is an award-winning author of fifteen books. Prior to his writing career, John was a university professor in both the United States and Mexico, a cattle rancher, Quarter Horse breeder, designer of mequite furniture, and served in the U.S. Navy during the Korean War.

"There is an authenticity in John Duncklee's voice that you don't find in other writers of the American West today. His characters are as lively as a wild mustang stallion, and as unpredictable as the weather. If you love a good story, treat yourself to John Duncklee."

— Johnny Boggs, award-winning author and recipient of the Western Heritage Wrangler and Spur Awards.

Printed in the United States
72867LV00004B/4-6